"Red, Please Don't Cry;

I'm sorry." The anger was gone and he spoke softly, reassuringly.

She shivered with reaction. "If . . . if we did get married, could I stay here until I finished my schooling?"

"I need a wife and children. Look at me, Red. I'm thirty-six. I can't wait another five, six years for a family. And I work too hard to divide my life between Nome and Seattle."

"You're asking for so much," she cried.

"But I'm offering even more," he countered.

"I can't give it all up. It's not that easy," she whispered.

"Then there's nothing left to say, is there?"

Dear Reader:

In times like these more and more people are turning to their faith. And they want to read about people like themselves, people who hold the same beliefs dear. If this sounds familiar, you might find that SILHOUETTE INSPIRATIONS are about people like you.

SILHOUETTE INSPIRATIONS are love stories with a difference—they are novels of hope and faith about people who have made a commitment or recommitment of their lives to Christ. And SILHOUETTE INSPIRATIONS are also wonderful romances about men and women experiencing all the joy of falling in love—romances that will touch your heart.

SILHOUETTE INSPIRATIONS—more than just a love story, a love story you'll cherish!

The Editors
SILHOUETTE INSPIRATIONS

THANKSGIVING PRAYER
Debbie Macomber

Silhouette Inspirations

Published by Silhouette Books New York

America's Publisher of Contemporary Romance

Inspirations by Debbie Macomber

Heartsong #1
Undercover Dreamer #9
A Girl Like Janet #15
Thanksgiving Prayer #21

SILHOUETTE BOOKS, a Division of Simon & Schuster, Inc.
1230 Avenue of the Americas, New York, N.Y. 10020

Distributed by Pocket Books

ISBN: 0-671-50357-X

First Silhouette Books printing November, 1984

10 9 8 7 6 5 4 3 2 1

America's Publisher of Contemporary Romance

Printed in the U.S.A.

Dedicated to
Marie Macomber,
Mother-in-law extraordinaire

THANKSGIVING PRAYER

Chapter One

The radiant blue heavens wooed Claudia Masters as she boarded the jet for Nome, Alaska. Her heart rate accelerated with excitement. In less than two hours she would be with Seth—manly, self-assured, masterful Seth. She made herself comfortable and secured the seat belt, anticipating the rumble of the mighty engines that would thrust the plane into the welcoming sky.

There had been some uncertainty when Claudia boarded the plane that morning in Seattle. But a hastily placed phone call from Anchorage, and she'd been assured by Seth's secretary that yes, he had received her message, and yes, he would meet her at the airport. Again confident, Claudia relaxed and idly flipped through a magazine.

A warmth, a feeling of contentment encompassed her. Cooper's doubts and the last-ditch effort to change her mind were behind her now, and she was free to make her life with Seth.

Cooper had been furious with her decision to leave medical school. But Cooper was only her uncle, even if he was the same age as Seth. He hadn't understood her love for the itinerant oilman, just as he couldn't understand her faith in the Lord.

A smile briefly curved her soft mouth upward. Cooper had shown more emotion in that brief twenty-minute visit to his office than she'd seen in all her twenty-two years.

"Quitting med school is the most stupid idea I've ever heard," he'd growled, the keen brown eyes challenging the serene blue of hers.

"Sometimes loving someone calls for unusual behavior," she had countered. Anything impractical was foreign to her uncle.

For a moment all Cooper could do was stare at her. She could sense the anger drain from him as he lowered himself into the desk chair.

"Contrary to what you may believe, I have your best interests at heart. I see you throwing away years of study for some ignorant lumberjack. Can you blame me for doubting your sanity?"

"Seth's an oilman, not a lumberjack. There aren't any trees in Nome." It was easier to correct Cooper than to answer the questions that had plagued her with doubts. The choice hadn't been easy; indecision had tormented her for months. Now that she'd decided to marry Seth and share his life in the Alaskan wilderness, a sense of joy and release came to her.

"It's taken me two miserable months to realize that my future isn't in any hospital," she continued. "I'd be a rotten doctor if I couldn't be a woman first. I love Seth. Someday I'll finish medical school, but if a decision has to be made, I'll choose Seth Lessinger every time."

But Cooper had never been easily won over. The tense atmosphere became suddenly quiet as he digested the thought. He expelled his breath, but it was several seconds before he spoke. "I'm not thinking of myself, Claudia. I want you to be absolutely sure you know what you're doing."

"I am." She smiled reassuringly, and for the first time since entering his office, she sat.

Now, flying high above the lonely, barren land of the Alaska tundra, Claudia was confident she was doing the right thing. God had confirmed the decision. It had taken her much longer to realize the truth, but Seth had known from the beginning.

Gazing out the plane window, she viewed miles upon miles of the frozen, snow-covered tundra. It was just as Seth had described: treeless plains of crystalline purity. There would be a summer, Seth promised, days firmly united when the sun would never set. Flowers would blossom, and for a short time the tundra would explode into a grassy pasture. Seth had explained many things about life in the North. At first she'd resented his letters, full of enticements to lure her to Nome. If he really loved her, he should be willing to relocate in Seattle until she'd completed her studies. It wasn't so much to ask. But as she came to know and love Seth, it became evident that Nome was more than the location of his business; it was a way of life, Seth's life. Crowded cities, traffic jams, shopping malls would suffocate him.

She should have known that the minute she pushed the cleaning cart into the motel room. Her being at the Wilderness Motel, cleaning rooms, was something of a miracle in itself.

Leaning back, Claudia slowly lowered her lashes as the memories washed over her.

Ashley Robbins, her lifetime friend and roommate, had been ill—far too sick to spend the day cleaning rooms. By the time Ashley had admitted as much, it was too late to call the motel and tell them she wouldn't be coming. Claudia had volunteered to go for her.

Claudia had known from the moment she slid the pass key into the lock. There was something special, something different about this room.

Her hands rested on slender hips as she surveyed the quarters. A single man slept here. A smile had trembled on her soft mouth as she thought of how accurate she was becoming at predicting the occupants of each room she cleaned. It had become a game to speculate who was here and why. Whoever had this room had rested uneasily. The sheet and blankets were ripped from the mattress and dumped haphazardly at the foot of the king-size bed.

As she stripped the sheets, Claudia couldn't help wondering what Cooper would think if he could see her now. He would be aghast to know she was doing menial work.

She lifted the corner of the mattress to tuck in the blanket, then felt as if someone had entered the room.

As she turned around, a smile lit up the sky-blue eyes. But her welcome died: no one was there.

Finishing the bed, she plugged in the vacuum. With the flip of the switch the motor roared to life. Again the sensation came and she turned off the machine. But when she turned, Claudia discovered she was alone.

Pausing, she studied the room. Silence encompassed her as she stood in the middle of the floor. There was something about this place: not the room itself, but the occupant. She could sense it, feel it, a depression, a sadness that seemed to reach out and touch her, wrap itself around her. Claudia wondered why she should be receiving these strange sensations. Nothing like this had ever happened to her before.

A prayer came to her lips as she silently petitioned God for whoever occupied this bed, this room. When she finished she released a soft sigh. Once, a long time ago, she remembered reading that no one could come to the Lord unless someone first prayed. Claudia wasn't sure how scriptural that was, but the thought had stuck with her. Often she found herself murmuring silent prayers for virtual strangers.

After cleaning the bathroom and placing fresh towels on the rack, she began to wheel the cleaning cart into the hallway. Again she paused, brushing wisps of copper-colored hair from her forehead as she examined the room. She hadn't forgotten anything, had she? Everything looked right. But again that terrible sadness seemed to reach out to her.

Leaving the cart, she moved to the desk and took out a postcard and a pen from the drawer. In large, bold letters she printed one of her favorite verses from Psalms. It read: "May the Lord give you the desire of your heart and make all your plans succeed." Psalm 20:4. She didn't question why that particular verse came to mind. It didn't offer solace, and yet it was unhappiness that she had felt. Perplexed and a little unsure, she placed the card in the metal prong that held the dresser mirror in place.

Outside, she checked to be sure the door had completeley closed and locked. Her back ached. Ashley hadn't been teasing when she said this was hard work. It was that and more. A thin sheen of perspiration wetted Claudia's brow, and she pushed the thick, naturally curly hair from her face. Her attention was focused on the door when she began wheeling the cart. She hadn't gone more than a few feet when she struck something. A quick glance upward told her she'd run into a man.

"Oh, sorry," she apologized immediately. "I wasn't watching where I was going." Her first impression was that this was the largest, most imposing man she'd ever seen. He loomed above her, easily a foot taller than her five-foot-five frame. His shoulders were wide, his waist and hips lean, and he was so muscular that the material of his shirt was pulled taut across the broad chest. He was handsome in a reckless-looking way, his hair magnificently dark. The full, well-trimmed beard was a shade lighter.

"No problem." The stranger smiled, his mouth sensuous and appealing, his eyes warm.

Claudia liked that. He might be big, but one look told her he was a gentle giant.

Not until she was in her car did Claudia realize she hadn't watched to see if the giant had entered the last special room.

By the time Claudia returned to the apartment,

Ashley looked better. Propped against the arm of the sofa, Ashley's back was cushioned with several pillows. A hand-knit afghan covered her legs and torso. A box of tissues sat on the coffee table, with crumbled ones littering the polished mahogany surface.

"How'd it go?" Ashley queried, her voice scratchy and unnatural. "Were you able to figure out one end of the vacuum from the other?"

"Of course." Claudia laughed. "I had fun playing the domestic, but next time warn me—I broke my longest nail."

"That's the price you pay for being so stubborn," Ashley scolded and grabbed a tissue, anticipating a sneeze. "I . . . I told you it was a crazy idea. Did old Burns say anything?"

"No, she was too grateful. Finding a replacement this late in the day would have been difficult."

Fall classes at the University of Washington had resumed that Monday, and Ashley had worked at the motel only a couple of weeks. Her friend hated to make a bad impression by calling in sick, so Claudia had offered to fill in for her at the last minute.

Claudia was pleased to help her friend. Her own school expenses were paid by a trust fund her father had established before his death. But Ashley maintained two part-time jobs to earn enough to stay in school. Claudia had offered to lend her friend money on numerous occasions, but Ashley had stubbornly refused. Ashley believed that if God wanted for her to have a teaching degree, then He would provide the necessary money. Apparently He did want that for her, because the funds were always there when she needed them.

Ashley's unshakable faith had taught Claudia valuable lessons. She had been blessed with material wealth while Ashley struggled from one month to the next. But of the two, Claudia considered Ashley the richer.

Often Claudia marveled at her friend's faith. Everything had been well taken care of in her own life. Decisions had been made for her. As for her career, she'd known from the time she was in grade school she would be a doctor. That dream had been shared by her father. The last Christmas before his death he'd given her a stethoscope. Later she realized that her father must have known he wouldn't be alive to see their dream fulfilled. Now there was only Cooper, her pompous, dignified uncle.

"How are you feeling?"

Ashley sneezed into the tissue that did little to muffle the sound. "Better," she murmured, her eyes red and watery. "I should be fine by tomorrow. I don't want you to have to fill in for me again."

"We'll see," Claudia said, hands on her hips and shaking her head. Stubborn Ashley, Claudia mused—she seemed to be surrounded by strong-willed, obstinate people.

Later that night, Claudia lay in bed unable to sleep. She hadn't told Ashley about what had happened in the last room she'd cleaned. She didn't know how she could explain it to anyone. Now she wished she'd waited to see if the stranger outside had been the one occupying that room. The day had been unusual in more ways than one. With a yawn, she rolled over and forced herself to relax and go to sleep.

The clouds were gray and thick the next morning. Claudia was up and reading over some material from one of her classes when Ashley strolled into the living room.

"Don't you ever let up?" she complained with a long yawn. "I swear all you do is study. Take a break, kid. You've got all quarter to hit the books."

With deliberate slowness Claudia closed the volume. "Do you always wake up so cheerful?"

"Yes," Ashley snapped. "Especially when I feel I could be dying. You're going to be a doctor—do something!"

Claudia picked up the thick book on psychology. "All right," she agreed. "Take two aspirin, drink lots of liquids and stay in bed. I'll check on you later."

"Wonderful," Ashley murmured sarcastically as she stumbled back into her bedroom. "And for this she goes to medical school."

A half hour later, Claudia tapped lightly before letting herself into Ashley's bedroom. "Feel any better?"

"A little." Ashley spoke in a tight voice. She was curled into a ball as if every bone ached.

"You probably have a touch of flu to go along with that rotten cold."

"This isn't a touch," she denied vehemently. "This is a full-scale attack. Why does this have to happen to me now?"

"Don't ask me," Claudia said as she set a tray of tea and toast on the nightstand. "But have you ever stopped to think that maybe your body has decided it needs a rest? You're going to kill yourself working at the motel and the bookstore, plus everything else. Something's got to give, and in this instance it's your health. I think you should take warning."

"Oh dear, here it comes." Ashley groaned and rolled over, placing the back of her hand to her forehead. "I wondered how long it would take to pull your corny doctor routine on me."

"It's not corny." The blue eyes flashed. "Don't you recognize good advice when you hear it?"

Ashley gestured weakly with her hand. "That's the problem, I guess. I don't."

"That's it," Claudia said and fluffed up a pillow so Ashley could sit up comfortably.

"I'm better, honest," Ashley said and coughed. "Good enough to work. I hate the thought of your breaking another fingernail."

"Sure you do, Ash, sure you do."

Claudia wheeled the cleaning cart from one room to the next without incident. The small of her back ached, and she paused to rub it. She hadn't done much housecleaning in her life. Ashley's mother had been their housekeeper and cook from the time Claudia was small.

Her fingers trembled when she inserted the pass key into the final room—the same one she had finished with yesterday. Would she feel the same sensations as before? Or had it all been her imagination? The room looked almost identical to the way it had been. The sheets and blankets were rumpled at the foot of the bed as if the man had slept restlessly.

Her attention flew to the mirror and she noted that the card was gone. Well, at least the occupant had discovered that. Slowly she walked around the quarters, waiting to feel the sensations she'd had yesterday. Whatever it had been was gone. Maybe she had conjured up the whole thing in her mind. The brain could do things like that. She should know. She'd studied enough about the human mind these past couple of days.

Claudia was placing the fresh white towels in the bathroom when a clicking noise was followed by the sound of the front door opening.

She stiffened as her fingers nervously toyed with the towel, pretending to straighten it.

"Hello." The male voice came from behind her, rich and deep.

"Hello," she mumbled and managed a smile. The man she had bumped into yesterday was framed in the doorway. Somehow Claudia had known he was the one occupying this room. "I'll be out of your way in a minute."

"No," he insisted. "Don't go, I want to talk to you."

Turning away from him, Claudia moistened her suddenly parched lips.

"Do I frighten you?" he asked.

Claudia realized that his size might intimidate many people. "No," she answered honestly. This man could probably lift a refrigerator by himself, yet he wouldn't hurt an ant. She wasn't sure how she knew this, but she did.

"Are you the one who left this?" He pulled the card she'd placed in the mirror from his shirt pocket.

Numbly she nodded. She didn't know anything about motel policy. This type of thing could possibly get Ashley into trouble.

His thick brows lifted as if he expected more than a simple shake of her head. "Why?" The single word seemed to be hurled at her.

"I . . . I don't really know," she began weakly,

surprised at how feeble her voice sounded. "If it offended you, then please accept my apology."

"I wasn't displeased," he assured her. "But I was a little curious about the reasons why." He released her gaze as he put the card back into his shirt pocket. "Do you do this often?"

Claudia looked away uneasily. "No. Never before."

His dark eyes narrowed on her. "Do you think we could have a cup of coffee somewhere when you're through? I really would like to talk to you."

"I . . ." She looked down on the uniform skirt the motel had provided and noted a couple of smudges.

"You look fine."

This stranger assumed she was a penniless motel maid. So many times Claudia had wished she could meet someone without the fear of intimidating him with her brains and position. Although she wasn't an heir to millions, she would receive a large cash settlement at age twenty-five, or the day she married —whichever came first.

"I'd like that." Obviously this stranger needed to speak to someone. The open Bible on his nightstand had convinced her he was a Christian. Was it because he was lonely that she had felt that terrible sadness in the room? No, she was sure it was more than loneliness—a lot more.

"Can we meet someplace?" he suggested. "There's a coffee shop around the corner."

"Fine," she said and nodded, knowing he had set the meeting in a public place so she would feel safe. Cooper would have a fit if he knew what she was doing. "I can be ready in about twenty minutes."

"I'll see you there." He stepped aside and Claudia could feel him studying her as she moved out of the bathroom. What was the matter with her? Never had she done anything so impulsive as meet a stranger like this.

With the room assignments finished, Claudia returned the cart to Mrs. Burns, who again thanked her. Next she made a stop in the ladies' room. One glance in the mirror and she groaned at the reflection. Her hair was an unruly mass of auburn curls. Taking the brush from her purse, she ran it through the long tresses until they sparked with electricity. Her thick, naturally curly hair had always been a problem. For several years now she had kept it long and pulled away from her face with a ribbon tied at the base of her neck. When she first applied and was accepted into medical school, she'd been determined to play down her femininity. Women weren't the rarity that they once were, but her sex combined with the money was sure to prejudice many of her classmates. There might have been some ill feelings her first year of medical school, but she had long since proved herself.

The coffee shop was crowded, but Claudia's searching gaze instantly located the stranger, who towered head and shoulders above the other patrons. Even when sitting, his large, imposing build couldn't be disguised. Weaving her way between chairs, Claudia sauntered toward him.

The welcome in his smile broke the smooth slant of his mouth. He stood and pulled out a chair for her. She noticed that he chose the one beside him as if he wanted her as close as possible. The thought didn't disturb Claudia, but her reaction to him troubled her. She wanted to be close to him.

"I suddenly realized I don't know your name," she said after sitting down.

"Seth Lessinger." A thick eyebrow arched in silent inquiry. "And yours?"

"Claudia Masters."

"I'm surprised they don't call you Red with that hair."

In any other family she might well have been tagged with the name, but not in hers. "No, I never was." Her voice contained a husky quality. To hide her discomfort, she lifted the menu and began studying its contents, although she didn't want anything more than coffee.

The waitress arrived and Claudia placed her order. Seth asked for a club sandwich.

"What brings you to Seattle?" she asked and absently smoothed a wrinkle from the skirt.

"A conference."

"Are you enjoying the Emerald City?" She was making small talk to cover up her nervousness. Maybe meeting a strange man like this wasn't such a good idea.

"Very much. It's my first visit to the Northwest, and I'll admit it's nicer than I expected. Big cities tend to intimidate me. I never have understood how anyone can live like this, among so many people."

Claudia didn't mean to smile, but amusement played at the edges of her mouth. "Where are you from? Alaska?" She'd meant it as a joke, but he nodded in confirmation.

"Nome," he supplied. "Where the air is pure and the skies are blue."

"You make it sound lovely."

"It's not," he told her with a half-smile. "It can be dingy and gray and miserable, but it's home."

Her coffee arrived and she cupped the mug, grateful to have something to do with her hands.

His eyes seemed to study her, and when their gazes clashed, a lazy smile flickered from the dark depths.

"What do you do in Nome?" His look was a gentle caress that Claudia found disturbing. Not that it made her uncomfortable: the effect was quite the opposite. He touched a softness in her, a longing to be the woman she had denied for so long.

"I'm a commissioning agent for a major oil company."

"That sounds interesting." She knew the words came out stiff and stilted.

"It's more than that. What about you?"

"Student at the University of Washington." She didn't elaborate.

A frown creased the wide brow. "You look older than a college student."

"I'm twenty-two." She concentrated her gaze on the black coffee. "How long will you be in Seattle?" If he noticed she was disinclined to talk about herself, he didn't say anything.

"I'll be flying back in a few days. I'd like to be home at the end of the week."

A few days, her mind echoed. She would remember to pray for him. Claudia believed that God brought everyone into her life for a specific reason. The purpose of her meeting Seth might be for her to remember to pray for him. He certainly had made an impression on her.

"How long have you been a Christian?" Seth inquired.

"Five years." That was another thing Cooper had

never understood. He found this "religious interest" of hers amusing. "And you?" Again she directed the conversation away from herself.

"Six months. I'm still an infant in the Lord, although my size disputes that!" He smiled, and Claudia felt mesmerized by the warmth in his eyes.

She returned his smile, aware he was as defensive about his size as she was about her money and her brains.

"Why'd you leave the Bible verse in the mirror?"

This was the crux of his wanting to talk to her. How could she explain? She didn't know why she'd done it. "Listen, I've already apologized for that. I realize it's probably against the motel policy."

A hand twice the size of her own reached over the table and trapped hers. "Claudia." The sound of her name was low-pitched and reassuring. "Don't apologize. The message meant more to me than you can possibly realize. My intention is to thank you for it."

The dark, mysterious eyes studied hers. Again Claudia sensed more than saw a sadness, a loneliness there. She made a show of glancing at her watch. "I . . . I really should be going."

"Can I see you again? Tomorrow?"

Claudia was afraid he was going to ask her that. Afraid he would, afraid he wouldn't.

"I was planning on doing some grocery shopping at the Pike Place Market tomorrow," she said without accepting or refusing.

"We could meet somewhere." His tone was clipped with a faint challenge. He sounded almost unsure. Claudia had the impression there wasn't much that unsettled this man. She wondered what it was about herself that caused him to be uncertain.

"All right," she found herself agreeing. "But I feel I must warn you, if you find large cities stifling, downtown Seattle at that time of the day may be an experience you'd wish to avoid."

"Not this time," he said with a chuckle.

They set a time and place as Seth walked her back to the motel and her car. Claudia drove a silver compact. Cooper had generously given her a fancy sports car when she was accepted into medical school. She'd never driven it around school and kept it in one of Cooper's garages. Not that she didn't appreciate the gift. The car was beautiful, and a dream to drive, but she already had her compact and couldn't see the need for two cars. Not when one of them would make her stand out and give her unnecessary and unwanted attention on campus. She told Cooper she couldn't keep it at the apartment because the color clashed with those of all the other cars in the parking lot. He had nodded in agreement. Cooper's whole life was color-coordinated, poor man.

"Hi." Claudia floated into the apartment, a Cheshire cat grin gently lifting her mouth into a smile.

"My heavens," Ashley groaned from the sofa. "You look like you've just met Prince Charming."

"I have." She dropped her purse on the end table and jumped up on the sofa arm the opposite end from Ashley. "He's about this tall." She held her hand high above her head. "With shoulders this wide." Her hands extended as far as they could reach from her sides. "And he has the most incredible dark eyes."

"Oh, honestly, Claudia, that's not Prince Charming. That's the Incredible Hunk," Ashley admonished on a sigh.

Claudia tilted her head to one side, a slow smile

spreading over her features. "Incredible is the word all right."

Not until the following morning, when Claudia dressed in her best designer jeans and cashmere sweater, with knee-high leather boots, did Ashley take her seriously.

"You really did meet someone yesterday, didn't you?"

Claudia nodded, pouring steaming cocoa into a mug. "Want some?"

"Sure," Ashley said and hesitated. "When did you have the chance? The only place you've been is school and"—she paused, her sky-blue eyes rounding—"the Wilderness and back. Claudia," she gasped, "it isn't someone from the motel, is it?"

Two pieces of toast blasted from the toaster with the force of a skyrocket. Deftly Claudia caught them in the air. "Yup."

For the first time in recent history, Ashley was speechless. "But, Claudia, you can't . . . I mean . . . all kinds of people stay there. He could be anyone. . . ."

"Seth isn't just anyone. He's large, so large he may shock you. But he's gentle and kind. I like him."

"I can tell," Ashley murmured with a worried look pinching her face.

"Don't look so shocked. Women have met men in stranger ways. I'm seeing him this afternoon. I told him I have some grocery shopping to do." At the glare Ashley was giving her, Claudia felt obliged to add, "Well, I do. I wanted to pick up some fresh vegetables. I was just reading an article on the importance of fiber in the diet."

"We bought a whole month's worth of food last Saturday," Ashley mumbled under her breath.

"True." Claudia shrugged. "But I think we could use some fresh produce. I'll be sure and pick up some prunes for you."

Seth was standing on the library steps waiting when Claudia arrived. Again she noted the compelling male virility. She waited on the bottom stairs for Seth to join her. A balmy September breeze coming off Puget Sound teased her hair, blowing the auburn curls across her cheek. Seth paused, standing in front of her, his eyes smiling deeply into hers.

The mesmerizing quality of his gaze held her motionless. Her hand was halfway lifted to her face to remove the lock of maverick hair, but it, too, was frozen by the warmth in his look, which seemed to reach out and caress her. Claudia had neither the will nor the desire to glance away.

The rough feel of his callused hand removing the hair brought her out of the trance. "Hello, Claudia."

"Seth."

"You're beautiful." The words appeared to come involuntarily.

"So are you," she joked. The musky scent of his cologne drifted pleasantly toward her, and an unwilling sigh broke from between her slightly parted lips.

Someone on the busy sidewalk bumped into Claudia, throwing her off balance. Immediately Seth's hand moved around her protectively. The iron band of his arm continued to hold her close, far longer than necessary. His touch warmed her through the thin jacket. No man had ever been able to produce this kind of feeling within her. This was uncanny, unreal.

Chapter Two

"Are you ready to call it quits?" Claudia questioned. Seth had placed a guiding hand at the base of her neck, and she wondered how long this touch would continue to produce the warm, glowing sensation that spread down her spine.

"More than ready," Seth confirmed.

The Pike Place Market in the heart of downtown Seattle had always been a hub of activity as tourists and everyday shoppers vied for the attention of the vendors who displayed their wares. Claudia and Seth strolled through the market, their hands entwined. Vegetables that had been hand-picked that morning were displayed on long tables, while the farmers shouted, enticing customers to their booths. The odd but pleasant smell of tangy spices and fresh fish drifted agreeably around them.

"I did warn you," she said with a small laugh. "What's the life expectancy rate of someone from Nome, Alaska, in crowds like this?"

Seth glanced at his wristwatch. "About two hours," he murmured. "And we've been at it nearly that. Let's take a break."

"I agree."

"Lunch?"

Claudia nodded. She hadn't eaten after her last class, hurrying instead to meet Seth. Now she realized she was hungry. "Sounds good."

"Chinese okay?"

For once it was a pleasure to have someone take her out and not try to impress her with the best restaurant in town, or how much money he could spend. "Yes, that's fine."

Seth paused. "You sure?"

She squeezed his hand. "Very sure."

They rode the city bus to Seattle's International Settlement and stepped off into another world. Seth looked around him in surprise. "I didn't know Seattle had a Chinatown."

"Chinatown, Little Italy, Mexico, all within a few blocks. Interesting, isn't it?"

"Very."

They lingered over the tea, delaying as long as possible their return to the hectic pace of the world outside.

"Why do you have a beard?" Claudia asked curiously. She didn't mean to be abrupt, but beards had always fascinated her.

Seth looked surprised by the question, rubbing both

sides of the dark hair with one hand. "Does it bother you? I can shave it off if you like."

"Oh, no," she protested instantly. "I like it. Very much. But I've always been curious why men sometimes chose to leave their beards."

"I can't speak for others, but growing one offers some protection to my face during the long winter months," he explained.

His quick offer to shave it off for her had faintly shocked Claudia. She couldn't understand his eagerness.

"I'm about finished my shopping. What about you?" She hated to torture him further.

The tiny teacup was dwarfed in his massive hands. "I was finished a long time ago."

"Want to take a walk along the waterfront and ride the trolley?" Claudia suggested, looking for reasons to prolong their time together.

"I'd like that."

While Seth paid for their meal she excused herself to reapply her lipstick and comb her hair. Then, hand in hand, they walked the short distance back to the heart of downtown Seattle. They paused at a major department store to study a window display in autumn colors.

Her eyes were laughing into his when Seth placed a possessive hand around her waist, drawing her close to his side. They stepped away from the window and started down the street toward the waterfront.

It was then that Claudia spotted Cooper walking across the opposite street. Even from this distance she could see the disapproving scowl on her uncle's face. The differences between these two men were so striking that to make a comparison would be ludicrous.

"I'll get us a taxi," Seth suggested, his eyes showing concern. "I've been walking your legs off." Apparently he thought her pale face was the result of the brisk pace he'd set.

"No, I'd rather walk," she insisted and reached for his hand. "If we hurry, we can make this light."

Their hands were linked when she began to run. There had never been any chance of their reaching the street before the light changed, but Claudia still proceeded to push between the busy shoppers.

"Claudia." Seth stopped, placing his arm over her shoulders, his wide brow creased with concern. "What's the matter?"

"Nothing," she said hesitantly, looking around her. She was certain Cooper had seen them. For once she didn't want him to ruin things. "Really, let's go." Her voice was raised and anxious.

"Claudia."

Cooper's voice behind her stopped her heart.

"Introduce me to your friend," Cooper requested in a crisp, businesslike tone.

Frustration washed over her. Cooper would take one look at Seth and judge him as one of the fortune hunters he was always warning her about.

"Cooper Masters, this is Seth Lessinger." The introduction was made grudgingly.

The two men eyed each other shrewdly while exchanging handshakes.

"Masters," Seth repeated. "Are you related to Claudia?"

Cooper ignored the question, instead turning toward Claudia. "I'll pick you up for dinner Sunday at about two. If that's convenient?"

"It was fine last week and the week before, so why should it be any different this week?"

Her uncle flashed her an impatient glance.

"Who is this man?" Seth questioned, the look in his eyes almost frightening. Anger darkened his face. He dropped his hand to his side, and she noted how his fist was clenched until the huge knuckles turned white.

Claudia watched, stunned. He thinks I'm Cooper's wife. Placing a hand on his forearm, she implored, "Seth, let me explain."

He shook his arm free. "You don't need to say anything more. I understand. Do you do this kind of thing often? Is this how you get your thrills?"

For a moment Claudia was speechless, the muscles of her throat paralyzed with anger. "You don't understand. Cooper's my uncle."

"And I believe in Santa Claus," Seth returned sarcastically.

"I've warned you about men like this." Cooper began speaking to her at the same time, confusing her.

"Will you please be quiet!" she shouted at her uncle.

"There's no excuse for you to talk to me in such a tone," Cooper countered in a huff.

People were beginning to stare, but Claudia didn't care. "He really is my uncle." Desperately her eyes pleaded with Seth, hers asking for understanding and the chance to explain. His were dark, clouded and unreasonable.

"You don't want to hear, do you?"

"We definitely need to have a discussion, Claudia," Cooper interrupted again.

"You're right, I don't." Seth took a step away from her.

Claudia breathed in sharply, the rush of oxygen inhaled so quickly her lungs hurt. She bit into her lip as Seth turned and walked away. His stride was filled with purpose, as if he couldn't get away from her fast enough.

"You've really done it this time," she flared at her uncle.

"Really, Claudia," he said with a relieved look. "That type of man is most undesirable."

"That man"—she pointed at Seth's retreating figure —"is one of the most desirable men I've ever known," she cried, stalking away.

An hour later, Claudia was banging pans around in the kitchen. Ashley came through the front door and paused, watching her for a moment. "What's wrong?"

"Nothing," Claudia responded shortly.

"Oh, come on. I always know when you're upset because you bake something."

"That's so I can eat it."

Ashley scanned the ingredients that lined the counter. "Chocolate chip cookies," she murmured. "This must really be bad. Obviously you had another run-in with Cooper?"

"Right again," Claudia snapped.

"You don't want to talk about it?"

"That's a brilliant deduction." With unnecessary force she cracked two eggs against the mixing bowl.

"You want me to leave?"

Claudia paused, closing her eyes as the waves of impatience rippled over her. "Ashley, please."

"All right, all right. I'm leaving."

Soon the aroma of freshly baked cookies filled the apartment, though Claudia didn't notice. Almost automatically she lifted the cookies from the baking sheet and placed them on a wire rack to cool.

"I can't stand it anymore." Ashley stumbled into the kitchen dramatically. "If you don't want to talk, fine, but at least let me have a cookie."

Claudia sighed, placed four on a plate and set it on the kitchen table.

Ashley poured herself a tall glass of milk and sat down, her eyes following Claudia's movements. "Feel like talking now?" she asked several minutes later. There was a sympathetic tone in her voice that came from many years of friendship.

Ashley had been Claudia's only friend as a child. Ashley's mother had been Claud Masters's cook and housekeeper. The woman had brought her daughter with her when she came to work, to keep the lonely Claudia company, and the two girls had been best friends ever since.

"It's Seth," Claudia admitted and sighed, taking a chair opposite Ashley.

"Seth? Oh, the guy you met at the motel. What happened?"

"We ran into Cooper, and he had a fit of righteous indignation to see me with someone not wearing a business suit and silk tie. To complicate matters, Seth apparently thought Cooper and I were married, or at least divorced. He didn't wait for an explanation."

Ashley's look was thoughtful. "You really like him, don't you?"

Claudia worried the soft flesh of her bottom lip. "Yes," she said simply. "I like him very much."

"If he's so arrogant that he wouldn't wait for you to explain, then I'd say it was his loss," Ashley attempted to assure her.

"No." Claudia shook her head and lowered her gaze to the tabletop. "In this case, I think I'm the one to lose."

"I don't think I've ever heard you talk this way about a man . . . anyone. What makes him so special?"

Claudia's brow knit in concentration. "I'm not really sure. He's more attractive than any man I can remember, but I'm not talking about looks. Although I think most women would think he was attractive. He's a rare man." She paused to formulate her thoughts. "Strong and intelligent."

"You know all this and you've only seen him twice?" Ashley sounded shocked.

"No." Claudia hung her head, and the long auburn curls fell forward. "I sensed more than saw, and even then that's only skimming the surface. This man is deep."

"If he's so willing to jump to conclusions, I'd say it's his own fault—"

"Ashley, please," Claudia interrupted. "Don't. I know you're trying to make me feel better, but I'd appreciate it if you didn't."

"All right." Ashley was quiet for a long time. After a while she took a chocolate chip cookie and handed it to Claudia.

With a weak smile, Claudia accepted the cookie. "Now, that's what I need."

They talked for a while, but it wasn't until Claudia entered the living room that she noticed Ashley's suitcase in front of the door.

"You're going away?"

"Oh, I almost forgot. I talked to Mom this morning, and she wants me home for a few days. Jeff and John have the flu and she needs someone there so she can go to work. I shouldn't be any more than a couple of days. You don't mind, do you?"

"Not at all," Claudia said with a smile. Although Ashley's family lived in the nearby suburb of Kent, Ashley lived with Claudia because it was easier for her to commute to school and back. But several times during the year she would move back home for a few days when her family needed her.

"You'll be all right, won't you?"

"Are you kidding?" Claudia joked. "The kitchen's full of cookies!"

Ashley laughed, but her large blue eyes contained a knowing look. "Don't be too hard on Cooper," she said and gave Claudia a small hug before she left.

What good would it do to be angry with her uncle? He was reacting the only way he knew how. Anger wouldn't help the situation.

The apartment felt large and lonely with Ashley gone. Claudia turned on the television and flipped through the channels, hoping to find something interesting, feeling guilty because she was ignoring schoolwork. Nothing. Good, she decided, and forced herself to hit the books. This quarter wasn't going to be easy, and the sooner she sharpened her study habits the better.

Two hours later she took a leisurely bath, dressed in a long purple velvet robe, curled up on the sofa and engrossed herself in a good book. Long ago she'd recognized that reading was her escape. When things were really bothering her, she'd plow through one mystery after another, not really caring about the characters or the plot so long as it was strong enough to distract her from her troubles.

The alarm rang at six and she stumbled out of bed, plugging in the coffeepot before stepping into the shower. As she rotated under the hot spray, her thoughts again drifted to Seth Lessinger. She felt some regrets. She would have liked to get to know him better. On Sunday she'd definitely have a talk with Cooper. She was twenty-two, old enough to choose who she wanted to date without his interference. It was bad enough being forced to endure a stilted dinner with him every Sunday afternoon.

She dressed in jeans, a plaid long-sleeved blouse and red sweater vest. Pouring herself a cup of coffee, she wondered how long she would have to force thoughts of Seth from her mind. The mystery novel had diverted her attention last night, but she couldn't live her life with her nose in a book. Today and tomorrow she would be busy with school, but it was Thursday and she wasn't looking forward to spending the evenings and weekend alone. She'd ask a friend at school if she'd like to go to a movie tonight.

She sat sipping from her mug at the kitchen table, her feet propped against the opposite chair, and read the morning paper. A quick look at her wristwatch and she placed the cup in the sink and hurried out the door for school.

Claudia pulled into the apartment parking lot later that afternoon. It seemed everyone had already made plans for this evening. Several of her friends were attending the Seahawk football game. Claudia loved football and decided to pop popcorn and stay at home and watch the game on television. She had no sooner let herself into the apartment and hung up her jacket when the doorbell rang.

The peephole in the door showed no one. It could be the neighbor's boy collecting for the jogathon. Claudia had sponsored the ten-year-old, who was trying to earn enough money for a soccer uniform. Todd had probably seen her pull into the parking lot. She opened the door and focused her gaze on the hallway.

"Claudia." Her name was breathed in surprise.

"Seth." Her heart tripped over itself.

"What are you doing here?" They both asked the question at the same time.

Claudia smiled. It was so good to see him, it didn't matter what the reason.

"I was looking for Ashley Robbins, the motel maid," he told her, the surprise leaving his eyes, to be replaced by a mocking glint.

"Ashley?" A pleasant warmth filled her. "Come in," she invited and closed the door after him. "Ashley's gone home for a few days to be with her parents. You don't know Ashley, do you?"

"No." One hand stroked the side of his beard. "But I was hoping she could tell me how to find you."

"We're roommates," Claudia explained unnecessarily. "You were looking for me? Why?"

Again Seth looked slightly ill at ease. "I wanted to

apologize for yesterday. I could at least have stayed and listened to an explanation."

"Cooper is my uncle."

"I should have known that. It wasn't until later that I realized I'd behaved like an idiot," Seth said, his face tight and drawn. "If I hadn't reacted like a jealous fool, I would have realized you would never lead anyone on like that."

"I know what you thought." She paused and glanced away. "I know how it looked, how Cooper wanted it to look."

Seth ran a self-derisive hand over his face. "Your uncle." He chuckled. Wrapping his arms around her, he lifted her off the ground and swung her around. Hands resting on the hard muscles of his shoulders, Claudia threw back her head and laughed.

Soon the amusement died as their gazes met and held. Slowly Seth released her until her feet had securely settled on the carpet. With an infinite gentleness, his hand brushed her face, caressing her smooth skin. It was so beautiful, so sweet, that Claudia closed her eyes to the sensuous assault. Her fingers clung to his arms as he drew her into his embrace, and her lips trembled, anticipating his kiss.

Seth didn't disappoint either of them as his mouth settled firmly over hers. His hand slid down her back, molding her against him, arching her upward to meet the demand of his kiss.

Claudia felt her limbs grow weak as she surrendered to the sensations swirling inside her. Her hands spread over his chest, but there was no resistance, only a rightness in the feel of his arms.

When he freed her mouth, his lips caressed the sensitive cord along the side of her neck.

"Does this mean you'll give me another chance?" He murmured the question, his voice faintly husky from the effects of the kiss.

"I'd say the prognosis is excellent," Claudia replied, her breathing still affected. "But I'd like to explain a few things."

She led the way into the kitchen, poured mugs of coffee and added sugar to his the way she'd seen him do. When she set his cup on the table, Seth reached for her hand and kissed her fingers.

"Your family has money?" he asked.

"Not me," she explained, "at least not yet. Cooper controls the purse strings for a little while yet. My father was Claud Masters; you may or may not have heard of him. He established a business supply corporation that has branch offices in five states. Dad died when I was in high school. Cooper is president of the company now, and my legal guardian." Her soft mouth quirked to one side. "He takes his responsibility seriously. I apologize if he offended you yesterday."

Humor glinted briefly in his expression. "The only thing that could possibly offend me is if you were married." He laughed and Claudia stared at him curiously. "I'll never wear five-hundred-dollar business suits. You understand that?"

Nodding, she smiled. "I can't imagine you in a suit at all."

"Oh, I've been known to wear one, but I hate it."

Again, Claudia smiled.

"Do you hate having money?" Seth was regarding her steadily, his wide brow creased.

"No," she replied honestly. "I can't say I dislike

money when I need it. What I hate is being different from others, like Ashley and you. I have a hard time trusting people. I'm never really sure they like me. I find myself looking at a relationship with a jaundiced eye, wondering what the other person is expecting to receive from my friendship." She lowered her gaze, her fingers circling the top of the mug. "My father was the same way. Consequently he closed himself off from the world. I was brought up in a protected environment. I fought tooth and nail to convince Cooper I should attend the University of Washington. He wanted to send me to study at a private university in Switzerland."

"I'm glad you're here."

Claudia watched as Seth clenched and unclenched his hands.

"Do you think the reason I came back is because you obviously have money?" he asked.

Something in his voice conveyed the seriousness of the question. "No, I don't think you're the type of person to be impressed by wealth. Just knowing you this little while, I believe if you wanted money, you'd have it. You're that type of man." Having stated her feelings, Claudia fell silent.

"God gives the very best." The throaty whisper was barely discernible, and Claudia glanced up, her blue eyes questioning.

"Pardon?"

Seth took her hand and carried it to his lips. The course hairs of his beard prickled her fingertips. "Nothing," he murmured. "I'll explain it to you later."

"I was going to fix myself a sandwich. Would you

like one?" she offered. "I guess I'm like a little kid coming home from school, needing my afternoon snack." Claudia had skipped lunch and suddenly realized she was hungry.

"I'd like that. You don't need to ask, I'm always hungry. Let me help," Seth volunteered. "Believe it or not, I'm a darn good cook."

"You can slice the cheese if you like." She flashed him a happy smile.

"I hope you don't have any plans for the evening," he said, easing a knife through the slab of cheese. "I've got tickets for the football game. The Seahawks are playing tonight and I . . ." He paused, his look brooding, disconcerted.

"What's wrong?"

Seth sighed, walked to the other side of the small kitchen and stuck his huge hands inside his pants pockets. "Football isn't much of a woman's sport, is it?"

"What makes you say that?" Claudia loved football.

"I mean . . ." He looked around uneasily. "You don't have to go. It's not that important. I know that someone like you isn't—"

Claudia didn't give him the chance to finish. "Someone like me," she repeated, "would love going to that game more than anything else." Her eyes were smiling into his.

Amusement dominated his face as he slid his arms around her waist. One hand toyed with a strand of her hair. "We'll eat a sandwich first, then grab something for dinner after the game. All right, Red?" He said the name as if it was an endearment. "You don't mind if I call you that, do you?"

"Only you," she murmured just before his mouth claimed hers. "Only you."

The day was wonderful. They spent a good portion of the afternoon talking, almost nonstop for two hours. Claudia, who normally didn't drink more than a cup or two of coffee, shared two pots with Seth. She told him things she had never shared with anyone: her feelings during her father's short illness and after his death; the ache, the void in her life afterward; and how the loss and the sadness had led her to Christ. She told him about her lifelong friendship with Ashley, the mother she had never known, medical school and her struggle for acceptance. There didn't seem to be anything she couldn't discuss with Seth.

In return he talked about his oil business, life in Nome and his own faith.

Before they knew it, the afternoon was gone. Claudia hurried to freshen up, but took the time to add a light perfume at her pulse points. Running a comb through the unruly curls that framed her face, she tied back the curls at the base of her neck with a silk scarf. Seth was waiting for her in the living room. Checking her appearance one last time, she noted the happy sparkle in her eyes and paused to murmur a special thank-you that God had sent Seth back into her life.

Seth helped her into her jacket. A rough hand ran lovingly up and down her arm as he brought her even closer to his side.

"I don't know when I've enjoyed an afternoon more," he told her. "Thank you."

"I should be the one to thank you, Seth." She

avoided eye contact, afraid how much her look would reveal.

"I knew the minute I saw you that you were someone very special. I didn't realize until today how right my hunch was." Seth looked down at her gently. "It wasn't so long ago that I believed Christians were a bunch of do-gooders. Not long ago I thought religion was for the weak-minded. But I didn't know people like you. Now I wonder how I managed to live my life without Christ."

A hand tugged Seth's as Claudia excitedly walked up the cement ramp of the Kingdome. "The game's about to start." They'd parked on the street, walking the few blocks to the stadium, hurrying up First Avenue. The traffic was so heavy that they were a few minutes late. The Seahawks were playing nationally televised games Monday nights, but this was Thursday. Claudia never hoped to understand the network's reasoning.

"I love football," she said, her voice unnaturally high with enthusiasm.

"Look at all these people." Seth stopped and looked around him in amazement.

"Seth," she groaned. "I don't want to miss the kickoff."

Because the football game was being televised back East, the kickoff time was slated for five o'clock Pacific time. More than sixty thousand fans filled the Kingdome to capacity. Seahawk fever ran high and the entire stadium was on its feet for the kickoff. In the beginning, Claudia applauded politely so she wouldn't embarrass Seth with her enthusiasm. But when it came to her favorite sport, no one could accuse her of being phlegmatic. Within minutes she was totally involved with the action of the players on the field. She'd cheer wildly, then shout at the officials in protest.

Seth's reaction was much more subdued, and several times when Claudia complained to him about a certain play or the refereeing, she found that Seth seemed to be watching her more closely than the game.

There was something about football which allowed her to be herself, something which broke down that natural reserve about her. With her school schedule, she couldn't take the time to attend the games. But if at all possible she watched them on TV, jumping on the furniture in exaltation, or pounding the carpet in despair. Most of her classmates wouldn't have believed it was the same girl. At school she was as serious as a schoolmarm, since she still felt the need to prove herself to her classmates. Although she had won respect from most of the other students, some still believed the only reason she had been accepted was her name and her sex.

"Touchdown!" Her arms flew into the air and she leaped to her feet.

For the first time since the game had started, Seth showed as much emotion as Claudia. Lifting her high, he held her tight against him. Her hands framed his face and it seemed the most natural thing in the world, staring into the dark, hungry eyes, to press her lips to his. Immediately Seth deepened the kiss, wrapping his arms around her, lifting her higher off the ground.

The cheering died to an excited chatter before either was aware of the crowd.

"We have an audience," Seth murmured huskily in her ear.

"It's just as well, don't you think?" Her face was flushed lightly. Claudia had known almost from the beginning that the attraction between them was stronger than anything she had experienced with another man. Seth seemed to have recognized this as well. The effect they had on each other was strong and disturbing. Seth had kissed her only three times, and already they were aware of how easy it would be to let their attraction rage out of control. It was exciting, but in another sense it was frightening.

After the game they stopped for hamburgers. When Seth had finished his meal, he returned to the counter and bought them each an ice cream sundae.

"When you come to Alaska, I'll have my Eskimo friends make you some of their ice cream," he said. His eyes flashed her a look of amusement.

Claudia's stomach tightened. *When* she came to Alaska? She hadn't stopped to think about ever visiting America's last frontier. From the beginning she had known that Seth would be in Seattle only a few days. She had known and accepted that as best she could.

Deciding it was best to ignore the comment, she cocked her head to one side. "Okay, I'll play your little game. What's Eskimo ice cream?"

"Berries, snow and rancid seal oil."

"Well, at least it's organic."

Seth chuckled. "It's that all right."

Claudia twisted the red plastic spoon, making circles in the soft ice cream. She avoided Seth's gaze, just as she had been eluding facing the inevitable.

Gathering her resolve, she raised her face, her eyes meeting his. "When will you be returning to Nome?"

Seth pushed his dessert aside, his hand reaching for hers. "My flight's booked for tomorrow afternoon."

Chapter Three

The muscles of Claudia's throat constricted. "To-morrow," she repeated, knowing she sounded like a parrot. Lowering her gaze, she continued, "That doesn't leave us much time, does it?" She'd thought she was prepared. Hadn't she known from the beginning that Seth would only be in Seattle for a few days?

Lifting her eyes to his watchful gaze, she offered him a weak smile. "I know this sounds selfish, but I don't want you to go."

"Then I won't," he announced casually.

Claudia's head shot up. "What do you mean?"

The full force of his magnetic eyes was resting on her. "I mean I'll stay a few more days."

Claudia's heart seemed to burst into song. "Over the weekend?" Eyes as blue as the Caribbean Sea implored him. "My only obligation is dinner Sunday with Cooper, but you could come. In fact, I'd like it if you did. My uncle will probably bore you to tears, but I'd like you to get to know each other. Won't you stay that long?" She tilted her head questioningly, hopefully.

Seth chuckled. Claudia loved the sound of his laugh. The loud, robust sound seemed to roll from deep within his chest. She'd watched him during the football game and couldn't help laughing with him.

"Will you?" She repeated the question.

"I have the feeling your uncle isn't going to welcome me with open arms."

"No." She smiled beguilingly. "But I will."

The restaurant seemed to go still, quiet. Seth's gaze was penetrating, his voice slightly husky. "Then I'll stay, but no longer than Monday."

"Okay." She was more than glad, she was jubilant. There hadn't been time to question this magnetic attraction that had captured them, and deep down Claudia didn't want to investigate her feelings, even though this was all happening too fast.

Seth's arm slipped around her waist as they walked to the car. He held open the door for her and waited until she was seated. Unconsciously her fingers smoothed the plush sheepskin cushions, their texture smooth against the tips of her fingers. The vehicle had surprised her. Seth didn't fit the luxury-car image.

"This thing is a bit much, isn't it?" His gaze briefly scanned the interior. The limousine was fitted with every convenience, from the automatic sunroof to a stereo system that must have cost thousands. Such opulence was an embarrassment to him. Claudia had seen her share of luxury cars, but this one surprised even her.

"Did you rent it?" she felt obliged to ask.

"Heavens, no! This is all part of the sisters' efforts to get me to sign the contract."

"The sisters?"

"That's a slang expression for the major oil conglomerates. They seem to feel the need to impress me. My original hotel reservation was at the Four Seasons, in a suite that was three hundred dollars a night. I wouldn't put up with that, and found my own place. But I couldn't refuse the car without offending some important people."

"We all get caught in that sometimes."

Seth agreed with a short, preoccupied nod. Although the football game had finished over an hour before, the downtown traffic was at a standstill. Cautiously Seth eased the limousine into the heavy flow of bumper-to-bumper traffic.

While they were caught in the snarl of impatient drivers, Claudia watched Seth's strong profile. Several times his mouth tightened and he shook his head in disgust.

"I'm sorry, Seth," she said solemnly and smiled lamely when he glanced at her.

He arched thick brows. "You're sorry? Why?"

"The traffic. I should have known to wait another hour, until things had thinned out a bit more."

"It's not your fault." His enormous hand squeezed hers reassuringly.

"Don't you have traffic jams in Nome?" she asked, partly to keep the conversation flowing, and partly to counteract the crazy reaction her heart seemed to have every time he touched her.

"Traffic jams in Nome?" He smiled. "Red, Nome's population is barely three thousand. On certain days my car is the only one on the road."

Claudia's eyes narrowed suspiciously. "You're teasing? I thought Nome was a major Alaskan city."

He returned both hands to the wheel and Claudia's heartbeat relaxed. "The population of the entire state is only 400,000, a mere fraction of Washington's four million." A smile softened the rugged features. "Anchorage is the largest city in Alaska, with about 200,000 residents."

"Washington's the closest state to Alaska, and even I didn't know that. I must have been daydreaming during geography class in the fifth grade."

An impatient motorist honked and Seth pulled forward onto the freeway entrance ramp. The traffic remained heavy but was moving at a steady pace.

"I couldn't live like this," he said and expelled his breath forcefully. "Too many people, too many buildings and," he added with a wry grin, "too many cars."

"Don't worry. You won't have to put up with it much longer," she countered with a smile.

Seth scowled thoughtfully and didn't reply.

He parked the car in the lot outside her apartment building and refused the invitation to come in for coffee. "I have a meeting in the morning that shouldn't go any longer than noon. Can I see you then?"

She nodded, pleased. "Of course." Every minute left would be treasured. "Shall I phone Cooper and tell him you're coming for dinner Sunday?"

"He won't mind?" Seth queried.

"Oh, I'm sure he will, but if he objects too strongly, we'll have our own dinner."

His hand reached out to caress the delicate curve of her cheek and entwine with the auburn curls along the nape of her neck. "Would it be considered bad manners to hope he objects strenuously?" he asked.

"Cooper's not so bad." Claudia felt as if she should at least make the effort to explain her uncle. "I don't think he means to come off so pompous, he just doesn't know how else to act. What he needs is a woman to love." She smiled inwardly. "I can just hear him cough and sputter if I were to tell him that."

"I need a woman to love," Seth whispered as his mouth found hers. The kiss was deep and intense, as if to convince her of the truth of his words.

Claudia wound her arms around his neck, surrendering to the mastery of his kiss. He's serious, her mind repeated, dead serious. Not that it mattered, not when she was in his arms. The whole world seemed right when Seth was holding her like this. He covered her neck and the hollow of her throat with light, tiny kisses. Claudia tilted her head at an angle reveling in the warm feel of his lips against the creamy smoothness of her skin. A shudder of desire ran through her, and she bit into her bottom lip to conceal the effect he had on her senses.

Taking in a deep breath, Seth straightened. "Let's get you inside before this gets out of hand." His voice sounded raw and slightly uneven.

He kissed her again outside her apartment door, but this one lacked the ardor of a few minutes earlier. "I'll see you about noon tomorrow."

With a trembling smile she nodded.

"Don't look at me like that," he groaned. His strong hands stroked the length of her arms as he edged her body closer. "It's difficult enough to say good night."

Standing on tiptoe, she lightly brushed her mouth over his.

"Claudia," he growled in warning.

She placed her fingertips over her moist lips, then over his, to share the mock kiss with him.

Seth closed his eyes as if waging some deep inner battle, then covered her fingers with his own.

"Good night," she whispered, glorying in the way he reacted to her.

"I'll see you tomorrow."

"Tomorrow," she repeated dreamily.

Dressed in her pajamas and housecoat, Claudia sat on top of her bed an hour later, reading her Bible. Her concentration drifted to the events of the past week and all the foreign emotions she had encountered. This thing with Seth was happening too fast, far too fast. No man had ever created such an intensity of emotion within her. No man had made her feel the things he did. Love, real love, didn't happen like this. The timing was all wrong. She couldn't fall in love—not now. Not with a man who was only going to be in Seattle for a few days. But why had God sent Seth into her life when it would be so easy to fall in love with him? Was it a test? A lesson in faith? She was going to be a doctor. The Lord had led her to that decision, and there wasn't anything in her life she was more sure of. Falling in love with Seth Lessinger could ruin that. Still troubled, she turned off the light and attempted to sleep.

Claudia was ready at noon, but for what she wasn't sure. Dressed casually in jeans and a sweater, she thought she might suggest a drive to Snoqualmie Falls. And if Seth felt ambitious, maybe a hike around Mount Si. Claudia didn't have the time to do much hiking herself, but she enjoyed the outdoors whenever possible. The mental picture of idly strolling with Seth, appreciating the beautiful world God had given, was an appealing one. Doing anything with Seth was appealing.

When he hadn't shown by one, Claudia became worried. Every minute seemed interminable, and she glanced at her watch repeatedly. When the phone rang at one-thirty, she grabbed the receiver after only one chime.

"Hello," she said anxiously.

"Red?" Seth asked.

"Yes, it's me." He didn't sound right; he seemed tired, impatient.

"I've been held up here. There's not much chance of my getting out of this meeting until late afternoon."

"Oh." She tried to hide the disappointment in her voice.

"I know, honey, I feel the same way." The depth of his tone relayed his own frustration. "I'll make it up to you tonight. Can you be ready around seven for dinner? Wear something fancy."

"Sure." She forced a cheerful note in her voice. "I'll see you then. Take care."

"I've got to get back inside. If you happen to think

of me, say a prayer. I want this business over so we can enjoy what's left of our time."

If she thought of him? Claudia nearly laughed out loud. "I will," she promised, and did.

Cooper phoned about ten minutes later. "You left a message for me to call?" he began with a question.

Claudia half suspected Cooper wanted her to apologize for the little scene downtown with Seth. "Yes," she replied evenly. "I'm inviting a guest for dinner Sunday."

"Who?" he asked, and Claudia could almost picture him bracing himself because he knew the answer.

"Seth Lessinger. You met him already once this week."

The line seemed to crackle with a lengthy silence. "As you wish," he said tightly.

A mental picture formed of Cooper writing down Seth's name. Undoubtedly, before Sunday, her uncle would know everything there was about Seth, from his birth weight to his high school grade point average.

"We'll see you then."

"Claudia," Cooper said and hesitated. Her uncle didn't often hesitate. Usually he knew his mind and wasn't afraid to speak it. "You're not serious about this"—he searched for the right word—"man, are you?"

"Why?" It felt good to turn the tables, answering her cagey uncle with a question of her own. Why should he be so concerned? She was twenty-two, old enough to do anything she pleased.

Cooper allowed an unprecedented second pause. "No reason. I'll see you Sunday."

Thoughtfully Claudia replaced the receiver and released her breath in a slow sigh. Cooper sounded different, on edge, not like his normal self at all. Her mouth quivered with a suppressed smile. Cooper was worried; she'd heard the concern in his voice. For the first time since he'd been appointed her guardian, he had showed some paternal feelings toward her. The smile grew. Cooper wasn't such a bad fellow after all.

Scanning the contents of her closet later that afternoon, Claudia chose a black lace dress she had bought on impulse the winter before. This wasn't the type of dress she'd wear to church, although it wasn't low-cut or revealing. Made of Cluny lace, the one-piece outfit had a three-tiered skirt. Claudia had seen it displayed in an exclusive boutique, but was angry with herself at the time for buying something so extravagant. She was unlikely to find a reason to wear a dress this elegant, but she'd loved it and couldn't resist. Even Ashley had been surprised when Claudia had showed it to her. No one could deny that it was a beautiful, romantic dress.

The auburn curls were formed into a loose chignon at the top of her head, with tiny ringlets falling at the sides of her face. The diamond earrings had been her mother's, and Claudia had worn them only a couple of times. Seth had said fancy, he was going to get fancy!

He arrived promptly at seven. One look at Claudia and his eyes showed surprise, then astonishment, then something else she couldn't decipher.

Slowly his gaze traveled over her face and figure, openly admiring the curved hips and slender legs.

"Wow."

"Wow yourself," she returned, equally impressed. Claudia saw him as a virile and intriguing male without the rich dark wool suit. But now he was compelling and so attractive she could hardly take her eyes off him.

"Turn around, I want to look at you," he requested, his attention centered on her. His voice sounded ragged, as if seeing her had stolen away his breath.

Claudia did as he asked, slowly twirling around. "Now you."

"Me?" He looked stunned.

"You." She laughed, her hands directing his movements. Self-consciously he turned, his movements abrupt and awkward. "Where are we going?"

"The Space Needle." He took the white coat out of her hands and held it open for her. Claudia turned and slid her arm into the satin-lined sleeves. Seth guided it over her shoulders, and his hands lingered there as he brought her back against him. She heard him inhale sharply before kissing the gentle slope of her neck.

"Let's go," he murmured, "while I'm able to resist other temptations."

Seth parked outside the Seattle Center and they walked hand in hand toward the city's most famous landmark.

"Next summer we'll go to the Food Circus," she mentioned casually. If he could say things that spoke of her visiting Alaska, she could toss out the same things at him.

Seth didn't miss a step, but his hand tightened over hers. "Why next summer? Why not now?"

"Because you've promised me dinner on top of the city, and I'm not about to let you out of that. But anyone visiting Seattle shouldn't miss the Food Circus. A multitude of booths serve exotic dishes from all over the world. The worst part is having to make a decision. When Ashley and I go there, we each buy something different and divide it. That way we both get a taste of something new." She stopped talking and smiled. "I'm chattering, aren't I?"

"A little." She could hear the amusement in his voice.

The outside elevators whisked them up the Space Needle to the observation deck 607 feet above the ground. The night was glorious; brilliant lights lit up the world below. Seth stood behind her, his arms looped over her shoulders, pressing her close.

"I think my favorite time to see this view is at night. I love watching all those lights. I've never stopped to wonder why the night lights enthrall me the way they do. But I think it's probably because Jesus told us we were the light of the world, and from up here I can see how much one tiny light can illuminate."

"I hadn't thought of it like that," Seth murmured close to her ear. "But you have to remember I'm a new Christian. There are a lot of things I haven't discovered yet."

"That's a wonderful part, too."

"How do you mean?"

She shrugged lightly. "God doesn't throw all this knowledge and insight at us at once. He lets us digest it little by little, as we're able."

"Just as any loving father would do," Seth said quietly.

They stood for several minutes until a chill ran over Claudia's arms.

"Cold?" he questioned.

"Only a little. It's so lovely out here, I don't want to leave."

"It's beautiful all right, but it's more the woman I'm with than the scenery."

"Thank you," Claudia murmured, pleased by his words.

Seth was still behind her. "You're blushing." The pressure of his arms turned her around. "I don't believe it—you're blushing."

Embarrassed, Claudia looked away. "Men don't usually say those things to me."

"Why not? You're a beautiful woman. By now you should have heard those words a thousand times over."

"Not really." The color was creeping up her neck. "That's the floating bridge over there." She pointed into the distance, attempting to change the subject. "It's the largest concrete pontoon bridge in the world. It connects Mercer Island and Seattle."

"Claudia," Seth murmured, his voice dipping slightly, "you are a delight. If we weren't out here with the whole city looking on, I'd take you in my arms and kiss you senseless."

"Promises, promises," she teased and hurried inside before he could make good his words.

They ate a leisurely meal and talked over coffee so long that Claudia looked around guiltily. Friday night was one of the busiest nights for the restaurant business.

"I'll make us another cup at my place," she volunteered.

Seth didn't argue.

The aroma of fresh-brewed coffee filled the apartment. Claudia poured them each a cup and carried it into the living room.

Seth sat on the long, green couch, flipping through the pages of one of the medical journals Claudia had stacked on the end table.

"Are you planning on specializing?"

She nodded. "Probably pediatrics."

His dark brown eyes became intent. "Do you enjoy children that much, Red?"

"Oh, yes," she said fervently. "Maybe it's because I was an only child and never got my fill. I can remember lining up my dolls and playing house."

"I thought every little girl did that?"

"At sixteen?" she teased, then laughed at the expression on his masculine face. "The last two summers I've worked part-time in a day care center to see how I'd interact with children. The experience convinced me to go into pediatrics. But that's a long ways down the road. I'm only a first-year medical student."

When they'd finished the coffee, she carried their cups to the kitchen sink. Seth followed her, slipping his hands around her waist. All her senses reacted to his touch.

"Can I see you in the morning?"

She nodded, afraid her voice would tremble if she spoke. His finger traced the line of her cheek and Claudia held her breath, bracing herself as it trailed over her soft lips. Instinctively her arms reached for him, gliding up his chest and over the corded muscles of his shoulders. The steel fibers flexed beneath her exploring fingers. He rasped her name before his mouth hungrily descended on hers. A heady excitement engulfed her. Never had there been a time in her life when she was more gloriously happy. The kiss was searing, turbulent, wrenching her heart and touching her soul.

"Red?" His hold relaxed and with infinite care he studied her soft, yielding eyes, filled with the depth of her emotions. "Oh, Red?" He inhaled several sharp breaths and pressed his forehead to hers. "Don't tempt me like this." The words were a plea that seemed to come deep from within him.

"You're doing the same thing to me," she whispered softly, having trouble with her own breathing.

"We should stop now."

"I know," she agreed, but neither pulled away from the other.

How could she think reasonable thoughts when he was so close? A violent eruption of Mount St. Helens couldn't compare with the ferocity of her emotions.

Slowly she pulled back, easing herself from his arms.

He dropped his hands limply to his sides. "We have to be careful, Red. My desire for you is strong, but I want us to be good. I don't think I could ever forgive myself if I were to lead us into sin."

"Oh, Seth," she whispered, her blue eyes shimmering with tears. "It's not all you. I'm feeling these things just as strongly. Maybe it's not such a good idea for us to be alone anymore."

"No." His husky voice rumbled with turmoil. A tortured silence followed. He paced the floor, raking his fingers through his thick brown hair. "It's selfish, I know, but there's so little time left. We'll be careful and help one another. It won't be much longer that we'll be able . . ." He let the rest of the sentence fade.

Not much longer, her mind repeated.

He picked up the jacket he'd discarded over the back of a chair and held out a hand to her. "Walk me to the door."

Linking her fingers with his, she did as he asked. He paused at the door, his hand on the knob. "Good night."

"Good night," she responded with a weak smile.

He bent downward and gently brushed her lips. Although the contact was light, almost teasing, Claudia's response was immediate. She yearned for the feel of his arms again and felt painfully empty when he turned away and closed the door behind him.

They spent almost every minute of Saturday together, their day full and varied. In the morning Seth drove them to Snoqualmie Falls and they ate a picnic lunch, then took a leisurely stroll along the trails leading to the water. Later in the day they visited the Seattle Aquarium on the waterfront and ate a dinner of fresh fish and crusty, deep-fried potatoes.

Cooper phoned to tell her Seth was welcome for Sunday dinner, a gesture that surprised her.

"He's a good man," Cooper announced. "I've been hearing quite a few impressive things about your lumberjack."

"Oilman," she corrected, amused.

"I'll apologize for my behavior the other day," Cooper continued.

"I'm sure Seth understands," she assured him.

Six days. She had known Seth for a total of six days, and yet it felt like a lifetime. Her feelings for him were well defined now. Other than a few cases of puppy love, she had never experienced the deep womanly yearnings Seth created within her. The attraction was sometimes so strong that it shocked them. Aware of their physical weaknesses, they'd carefully avoided situations that would tempt them both. Now, although Seth touched her often and made excuses to caress her, he was cautious, and their kisses were never allowed to deepen into the passion they'd shared the night they dined at the Space Needle.

On Sunday morning Claudia woke early, with the eagerness of a child. The past week had been her happiest since before her father's death.

Claudia and Seth attended the early morning church service together, and she introduced him to her Christian family. Her heart filled with emotion as Seth sat beside her in the wooden pew. There could be nothing more she would ask in a man than a deep, committed faith in the Lord.

Afterward they went back to her apartment. The table was set with her best dishes and linen. Now she set out fresh-squeezed orange juice and delicate butter croissants on china plates. A single candle and dried-flower centerpiece decorated the table.

Claudia had chosen a pink dress and piled her hair high upon her head, with tiny curls falling free to frame her face. Although Seth would be leaving tomorrow, she didn't want to face that now, and quickly dismissed the thought. Today was special, their last day together, and she refused to let the reality of a long separation trouble her.

"I hope you're up to my cooking," she said to him as she tied the apron around her waist and took the special egg casserole from the oven.

Seth stood framed in the doorway, handsome and vital. He still wore a dark wool suit but held the restraining tie in one hand as if he didn't want the confining material around his neck any longer than absolutely necessary.

Just having him this close made all her senses pulsate with happiness, and a warm glow stole over her.

"You don't need to worry. My stomach can handle just about anything," he teased gently. He studied her for a moment. "I can't call you Red in a dress like that." He came to her and kissed her lightly. Claudia sighed at the sweetness of his caress.

"I hope I don't have to wait much longer; I'm starved."

"You're always hungry," she admonished. "Besides, how can you think about food when I'm here to tempt you?"

"It's more difficult than you know," he said with a smile. "Can I do anything?"

Claudia answered him with a short shake of her head.

"Well, are you going to feed me or not?" His roguish smile revealed stark masculinity.

The special baked egg recipe was one Ashley's mother had given her. Claudia was pleased when Seth asked for seconds.

"Here." Seth took a small package from his coat pocket. "This thing has been burning a hole in my pocket all morning. Open it now."

Claudia took the package and shook it, holding it close to her ear. "For me?" she asked, her eyes sparkling with excitement.

"I brought it with me from Nome."

From Nome? her mind questioned. Carefully she

untied the bow and removed the red foil paper, revealing a black velvet jeweler's box.

"Before you open it, I want to explain something." He leaned forward, resting his elbows on the table. "For a long time I've been married to my job, building my company. It wasn't until . . ." He hesitated. "I won't go into the reason, but I decided I wanted a wife. Whenever I needed anything in the past, I simply went out and bought it. I didn't think finding a good woman would work like that. It had to be someone special, someone I could love and respect, someone who shared my faith. The more I thought about the complexities of finding a wife, the more I realized how difficult it would be."

"Seth—"

"No, let me explain," he continued, reaching for her hand. He gripped it hard, his gaze studying her intently. "I was reading my Bible one night and came across the story of Abraham sending a servant to find a wife for Isaac. Do you remember the story?"

Claudia nodded, color draining from her features. "Seth, please—"

"There's more; bear with me." He raised her hand to his lips and very gently kissed her fingers. "If you remember, the servant did as Abraham bid and traveled to the land of his master's family. But he was uncertain, the weight of his responsibility bore heavily upon him. So the servant prayed, asking God to give him a sign. God answered that prayer and showed the servant that Rebekah was the right woman for Isaac. Scripture says how much Isaac loved his wife, and how she comforted him after the death of his mother, Sarah."

"Seth, please, I know what you're going to say—"

"Be patient, my love," he interrupted her again. "After reading that account, I decided to trust the Lord to give me a wife. I was also traveling to the land of my family. Both my mother and father originally came from Washington State. I prayed about it. I also purchased the engagement ring before I left Nome. And I, too, asked God for a sign. I was beginning to lose hope; I'd already been here several days before you placed the card with the verse in the mirror. You can't imagine how excited I was when I found it."

Claudia swallowed tightly, recalling his telling her that the message had meant more to him than she'd ever know. She wanted to stop him, but the lump in her throat had grown so large that speaking was impossible.

"I want you to come back to Nome with me tomorrow, Red. We can be married a few days later."

Chapter Four

Claudia's eyes widened with incredulous disbelief. "Married in a few days?" she repeated. "But, Seth, we've only been together six days! We can't—"

"Sure we can," he countered, his eyes serious. "I knew even before I found the Bible verse in the mirror that it was you. Do you remember how you bumped into me that first day in the outside corridor?" Although he asked the question, he didn't wait for the answer. "I was stunned. Didn't you notice how my eyes followed you? Something came over me right then. I had to force myself not to run and stop you. At the time I assumed I was physically reacting to a beautiful woman. But once I found the Bible verse on the mirror, I knew."

"What about school?" Somehow the words made it past the large knot constricting her throat.

A troubled look pinched his mouth. "I've done a lot of thinking about that, it's weighed heavily on me. I know how much getting your degree means to you." He caught her hand and gently kissed the palm. "Someday, Red, we'll be able to move to Anchorage and you can finish your schooling. I promise you that."

Taking her hand from his, Claudia closed the jeweler's box. The clicking sound seemed to be magnified a thousand times, a cacophony of sound echoing around the room.

"Seth, we've only known one another a short time. So much more goes into building the foundation for a relationship that will support a marriage. It takes more than a few days."

"Rebekah didn't even meet Isaac, she responded in faith, going with the servant to a faraway land to a man she had never seen. Yet she went," Seth argued.

"You're being unfair," Claudia said as she stood and walked to the other side of the room. Her heart was pounding so hard she could feel the blood pulsating through her veins. "We live in the twentieth century, not biblical times. How do we know what Rebekah was feeling? Her father was probably the one who said she would go. More than likely, Rebekah didn't have any choice in the matter."

"You don't know that," Seth said.

"You don't either," she shot back. "We hardly know each other."

"You keep saying that! What more do you need to know?"

Claudia gestured weakly with her hands. "Everything."

"Come on, Red. You're overreacting. You know more about me than any other woman ever has. We've done nothing but talk every day. I'm thirty-six, own and operate the Arctic Barge Company, wear size thirteen shoes, like ketchup on my fried eggs and peanut butter on my pancakes. My tastes are simple, my needs few. I tend to be impatient, but God and I are working on that. Usually I don't anger quickly, but when I do, stay clear. After we're married, there will probably be several things we'll need to discuss, but nothing we shouldn't be able to settle."

"Seth, I—"

"Let me see," he continued undaunted. "Did I leave anything out?" He paused again. "Oh yes. The most important part is that I love you, Claudia Masters."

The sincerity with which he said the words trapped the oxygen in her lungs, leaving her speechless.

"This is the point where you're supposed to say, 'And I love you, Seth.'" He rose, coming to stand directly in front of her. His hands cupped her shoulders as his gaze fell lovingly upon her. "Now repeat after me: *I . . . love . . . you.*"

Claudia couldn't. She tried to say something, but nothing would come. "I can't." She choked out the words. "It's unfair to ask me to give up everything I've worked so hard for. "I'm sorry, Seth, really sorry."

"Claudia!" His mouth was strained and tight; there was no disguising the bitter disappointment in his voice. "Don't say no, not yet. Think about it. I'm not leaving until tomorrow morning."

"Tomorrow morning." She closed her eyes. "I'm supposed to know by then?"

"You should know now," he whispered.

"But I don't," she snapped. "You say that God gave you a sign that I was to be the wife He had chosen for you. Don't you find it the least bit suspicious that God would say something to you and *nothing* to me?"

"Rebekah didn't receive the sign," he explained rationally. "The servant was the one. She followed in faith."

"You're comparing two entirely different times and situations."

"What about the verse you stuck in the mirror. Haven't you ever wondered about that? You told me you'd never done anything like that before."

"But . . ."

"You have no argument, Red."

"I most certainly do."

"Can you honestly say you don't feel the electricity between us?"

How could she? "I can't deny it, but it doesn't change anything."

Seth smoothed a coppery curl from her forehead, his touch gentle, his eyes imploring. "Of course it does. I think that once you come to Nome you'll understand."

"I'm not going to Nome," she reiterated forcefully. "If you want to marry me, then you'll have to move to Seattle. I won't give up my dreams because of a six-day courtship and the whim that you received a sign from God."

Seth looked shocked for a moment, but recovered

quickly. "I can't move to Seattle. My business, my home, my whole life are in Nome."

"But don't you understand that's exactly what you're asking me to do? My schooling, my home, my friends are in Seattle."

Seth glanced uncomfortably around the room, then directed his gaze back to her. His dark eyes were filled with such deep emotion, it nearly took Claudia's breath away. Tears shimmered in her eyes, and his tall, masculine figure blurred as the moisture welled.

Gently Seth took her in his arms, holding her head to his shoulder. His jacket felt smooth and comforting against her cheek. Taking in a quivering breath, she tried to stop the tears before they ruined her makeup.

Tenderly his hand caressed her neck and she could feel his breath against her hair. "Red, I'm sorry," he whispered with such love that fresh tears weaved a crooked course down her wan cheek. "I've known all this from the first day. It's unfair to spring it on you at the last minute. I know it must sound crazy to you now. But think about what I've said. And remember that I love you, nothing's going to change that. Now dry your eyes and we'll visit your uncle; I promise not to mention it again today." He kissed the top of her head and gently pulled away.

"Here." She handed him the jeweler's box.

"No." He shook his head. "I want you to keep the ring. You may not feel like you want it now, but you will soon. I have to believe that, Red."

Her face twisted with pain. "I don't know that I should."

"Yes." Brief anger flared in his eyes. "Please."

Because she couldn't refuse without hurting him

more, Claudia agreed with an abrupt shake of her head.

Since she didn't feel as if she could wear the ring, she placed the velvet box in a drawer. Her hand trembled when she pushed the drawer back into the dresser, but she put on a brave smile when she turned toward Seth.

To her dismay, his returning smile was just as weak.

Cooper knew something was wrong almost immediately. That surprised Claudia, who hadn't expected her uncle to be sensitive to her moods. But when he asked what was troubling her, she quickly denied that there was anything. Claudia couldn't expect Cooper to understand what was happening.

The two men eyed each other like wary dogs who had crossed paths unexpectedly. Cooper, for his part, was welcoming, but Seth was brooding and distant most of the day.

When they sat down to dinner, Seth smiled ruefully.

"What's wrong?" Claudia asked.

"Nothing," he said, shaking his head. "It's just this is the first time I've needed three spoons to eat one meal."

Cooper arched thick brows expressively, as if to say he didn't know how anyone could possibly do without three spoons for anything.

Claudia looked from one to the other, noting the differences. Two men from separate worlds. Although she found Cooper's attitudes and demeanor often boring and stringent, she was, after all, his own flesh and blood. If she were to marry Seth, give up everything that was important to her and move to Alaska, could she adjust to his way of life?

During the remainder of the afternoon, Claudia often found her gaze drawn to Seth. Cooper and Seth played a quiet game of chess in Cooper's den. Claudia sat opposite them, studying the two men.

Seth was the kind of man to thrive on challenges; he wasn't afraid of hardships. He was self-assured, and although she had never seen the ruthless side of his nature, Claudia didn't doubt that it existed. In the few days they had spent together she had been witness to the underlying thread of tenderness that ran through this man's heart. Seth thrived on hardships and challenges, but would she?

Resting her head against the velvet swivel rocker, she slowly lowered her gaze. The problem was she also knew that Seth was the type of man who loved intensely. His love hadn't been offered lightly; he wanted her forever. But most of all, he wanted her now—today. At thirty-six he had waited a long time to find a wife. His commitment was complete. He had looked almost disbelieving when she hadn't felt the same way.

Or did she? She couldn't deny that the attraction was powerful, almost overwhelming. But that had been physical, and there was so much more to love than the physical aspect. Spiritually they shared the same faith. To Claudia that was vital; she wouldn't share her life with a man who didn't believe as she did. But mentally they were miles apart. Each had goals and dreams that the other would never share. Seth seemed to believe medical school was a pastime, a hobby, with her. He had no comprehension of the years of hard work and study that had gotten her this far. The dream had been ingrained in her too long for her to relinquish it on the basis of a six-day courtship. And it wasn't only her dream, but one her beloved father had shared.

Seth hadn't understood any of this. Otherwise he wouldn't have asked her to give it all up without a question or thought. He believed that God had shown him she was to be his wife. If only life were that simple! Seth was a new Christian, eager, enthusiastic, but also a bit immature—not that she was a tower of wisdom and discernment. But Claudia would never have prayed anything so crazy. She was too down to earth, like Cooper. She hated to compare herself with her uncle, but in this instance it was justified.

Cooper's smile became faintly smug, and Claudia realized he was close to putting Seth in check, if not checkmate. Claudia didn't need to be told that Seth's mind was preoccupied with their conversation this morning and not on the chess game. Several times in the last hour he had lifted his gaze to hers. One look could reveal so much. Until that day, Claudia had never been aware how much Seth's eyes could say. He wanted her so much, more than he would ever tell. Guiltily her lashes fluttered downward; watching him was hurting them both too much.

He kissed her good night outside her apartment, thanking her for the day. A lump blocked her throat from thanking him for the beautiful solitaire diamond she would probably never wear.

"My flight's due to take off at seven," he said without looking at her.

"I'll be there," she whispered.

He held her then, so tight, that for a moment it was impossible to breathe. She felt him shudder, and tears prickled her eyes as he whispered, "I love you, Red."

She couldn't say it; couldn't repeat the words he desperately longed to hear. She bit into her tongue to keep from sobbing. She longed to tell him how she felt, but the words wouldn't come. They stuck in her throat until it constricted painfully and felt raw. Why had God given her a man who could love her so completely, when she was so wary?

Claudia set the alarm for five. If Seth's flight took off at seven, then she should meet him at the airport at six. She'd volunteered to drive him there, but he declined the invitation. He would take a taxi, somehow she knew it. Meeting him at Sea-Tac International would be far easier for Seth than her driving him there.

Sleep didn't come easily, and when it did, her dreams were filled with questions. Although she searched everywhere, she couldn't find the answers.

Her blue eyes looked haunted and slightly red the next morning. Claudia tried to camouflage the effects of the restless night with cosmetics.

The morning was dark and drizzly as she climbed inside her compact and started the engine. The car heater soon took the bite out of early morning, and she pulled onto the street. With every mile her heart grew heavier. A prayer came automatically to her lips. She desperately wanted to do the right thing: right for Seth, right for her. She prayed that if her heavenly Father wanted her to marry Seth, then He would make the signs as clear for her as He'd apparently done for Seth. Did she lack faith?

"No," she answered her own question aloud. But

her heart seemed to respond with a distant "yes" that echoed through her ears.

She parked in the garage, pulled her purse strap over her shoulder and hurried along the concourse. "I'm doing the right thing," she mentally repeated with each step. Her heels clicked against the marble floor, seeming to pound out the message—right thing, right thing, right thing.

After she'd passed through the metal detector and was free to join Seth, her pace quickened. She paused when she saw him and the dejected figure he made. Biting into her lip, she whispered a prayer, seeking strength and wisdom.

"Morning, Seth," she greeted him, forcing herself to smile.

His expression remained bland as he purposely looked away from her.

This was going to be more difficult than she imagined. The atmosphere was so tense and strained, Claudia couldn't tolerate it. "You're angry, aren't you?"

"No," he responded dryly. "I've gone beyond the anger stage. Disillusioned, perhaps. You must think I'm a crazy man, showing up with an engagement ring and the belief that God had given me this wonderful message that we were to marry."

"Seth, no." She placed a hand on his forearm.

He looked down at it and moved his arm, breaking her light hold. It was almost as if he couldn't tolerate her touch.

"The funny thing is," he continued, his expression stoic, "until this minute I didn't accept that I'd be returning to Alaska alone. Even as late as this morning I believed that something would happen and you'd decide to come with me." He took in a deep breath, his gaze avoiding hers. "I've behaved like a fool."

"Don't say that," she pleaded.

He glanced at her then; regret, doubt and a deep sadness touched his face. "We would have had beautiful children, Red." A hand lightly caressed her cheek.

"Will you stop talking like that," she demanded, becoming angry. "You're being unfair."

He quirked his head at an angle and shrugged his massive shoulders. "I know. You love me, Red, you haven't admitted it to yourself yet, but you do. The time will come when you can, but I doubt that even then it will make much difference. Because, although you love me, you don't love me enough to leave all this behind." His face scanned the airport interior, looking far beyond the glass, marble and concrete.

She wanted to argue with him, but couldn't. Unbidden tears welled in the blue depths of her eyes, and she lowered her head, blinking frantically to still their fall.

"Until you can admit your love for me, or anyone else, you'll only be half a woman. And when you stop putting your own dreams above everyone and everything—including God—then there's the chance you'll be a complete person."

The words seemed to reach out and physically slap Claudia. Her eyes widened incredulously, knowing they had been spoken with the intent to cause her pain.

She held her head high and glared at him with all the anguish in her eyes for him to see. "I'm going to forgive you for that, Seth, because I know you don't mean it. You're hurting, and because of that you want me to suffer, too." Tugging the leather purse strap over her shoulder, she took a step in retreat. "I can't see that my being here is doing either of us any good. I wish you well and thank you for six of the most wonderful days of my life. God bless you, Seth." She pivoted and stalked down the corridor. For several moments she was lost in a painful void. Somehow she managed to make it to a ladies' rest room.

Avoiding the curious stares of others, she wiped the moisture from her face and blew her nose. Seth had been cold and cruel, offering neither comfort nor understanding. Before, Claudia had recognized that his capacity for ruthlessness was as strong as his capability for tenderness. How sad that they must part like this. There'd been so much Claudia had longed to say, yet maybe it was better left unsaid.

When she felt composed enough to face the outside world, she moved with quick, purposeful steps toward the parking area.

She had only gone a few feet when a hand gripped her shoulder and whirled her around. A cry of alarm was muffled as she was dragged against Seth's muscular chest.

"I thought you'd gone," he whispered into her hair, a desperate edge to his voice. "I'm sorry, Red. You're right, I didn't mean that, none of it."

She was squeezed so tight her ribs ached. Seth raised his head and looked around at the attention they were receiving. A hand tugged her elbow and she was half dragged, half pulled into an area reserved for traveling servicemen. Thankfully it was empty. The minute he was assured they were alone, his mouth sought hers, fusing them together with a fiery kiss filled with such emotion that Claudia was left weak and light-headed.

"I need you," he whispered hoarsely against the delicate hollow of her throat. "God help me, I need you." He lifted his face and smoothed a curl from her forehead, his eyes pleading with her.

Claudia was deluged with fresh pain. She needed him too, but here in Seattle. She couldn't leave everything behind, not now, when she was so close.

"No, don't say it." He placed a finger over her mouth to prevent the words of regret from spilling out. "I understand, Red. Or at least I'm trying to understand." He sighed heavily and gently kissed her again. "I have to go—it's time to board the plane." His voice was low and troubled.

He sounded so final, as if everything between them was over. Claudia blinked away the tears that were burning her eyes. No sound came from her parched throat as she was gently eased from his embrace. Her heart hammered furiously as they returned to the departure gate.

A feeling of panic overcame her when she saw that Seth's plane was already being boarded. The time was fast approaching when he would be gone.

Once again he gently caressed her face, his dark eyes burning into hers.

"Good-bye, Red." His lips covered hers very gently. In the next instant, Seth Lessinger turned and strolled out of Claudia's world.

Part of her screamed silently in tortured protest as she watched him go, offering no resistance. The other part, the more level-headed, sensible part, recognized that there was nothing she could do to change his leaving. But all of Claudia suffered. Instantly she felt regret, remorse and self-reproach, but she found very little solace in her decision.

The days passed slowly and painfully. Ashley grew watchful over Claudia's loss of appetite and the dark shadows beneath her eyes. She spent more time in her room alone, blocking out the world, but closing the door on reality didn't keep away the image or the memories of Seth at bay. He was in her thoughts continually, haunting her dreams, obsessing her days, preying on her mind.

She threw herself into her studies with a ferocity that surprised even Ashley. The days she could handle, but not the nights. Often she lay awake for hours, wide-eyed and frustrated, afraid that once she did sleep her dreams would be haunted by Seth. She prayed every minute, it seemed, harder than she had about anything in her life. But no answer came: no flash of lightning, no writing on the wall, not even a Bible verse stuck to a mirror. Nothing. Wasn't God listening? Didn't He know that this indecision was tormenting her?

Two weeks after Seth's departure, she still hadn't heard from him. Claudia was hollow-eyed and her cheeks were beginning to look gaunt. Many times she saw Ashley glance at her with concern, but Claudia put on a weak smile and dismissed her friend's worries. No, she was fine. Really.

The next Saturday, Ashley was getting ready to go to work at the University Book Store near the U. of W. campus when one of the girls Ashley worked with, Sandy Hoover, waltzed into the apartment.

"Look." She proudly beamed and held out her hand, displaying a small diamond.

"You're engaged!" Ashley squealed with delight.

"Jon asked me last night," Sandy burst out. "I was so excited I could hardly talk. First, like an idiot, I started to cry, and Jon didn't know what to think. But I was so happy, I couldn't help it, and then I wasn't even able to talk and Jon finally asked me if I wanted to marry him or not and all I could do was emphatically nod my head."

"Oh, Sandy, I'm so happy for you." Ashley threw her arms around her friend and hugged her. "You've been in love with Jon for so long."

Her happy smile was animated. "I didn't ever think he'd ask me to marry him. I've known so much longer than Jon how I felt, and it was so hard to wait for him to feel the same things." She sighed, and a dreamy look stole over the pert face. "I love Jon so much it almost frightens me. He's with me even when he isn't with me." She giggled. "I know that sounds crazy."

It didn't sound so crazy to Claudia. Seth was thousands of miles away, but in some ways he had never left. If anything was crazy, it was the way she could close her eyes and feel the taste of his mouth over hers. It was the memory of that last gentle caress and the sweet kiss that was supposed to say good-bye.

Claudia was so caught up in her thoughts she hadn't noticed that Sandy had left.

"I wish you could look at yourself," Ashley said impatiently, her look thoughtful. "You look so miserable that I'm beginning to think you should see a doctor."

"A doctor isn't going to be able to help me," she mumbled.

"You've got to do something; you can't sit around here moping like this. It isn't like you, Claudia. Either you settle whatever's wrong between you and Seth or I'll contact him myself."

"You wouldn't," Claudia insisted.

"Don't count on it. Cooper's as worried about you as I am. If I don't do anything, he might."

"It isn't going to do any good." She tucked her chin into her neck. "I simply can't do what Seth wants. Not now."

"And what does he want?"

"He wants me to marry him and move to Nome," she whispered weakly. "But I can't give up my dream of a medical degree and move to some forsaken no-man's-land. And Seth just as adamantly refuses to move to Seattle. As far as I can see, there's no solution."

"You ninny," Ashley flared incredulously. "The pair of you! You're both behaving like spoiled children, each wanting your own way. For heaven's sake, does it have to be so intense? You've only known each other a few days. It would be absurd to make such a drastic change in your life on such a short acquaintance. And the same thing goes for Seth. The first thing to do is be sure of your feelings—both of you. Get to know each other better and establish a friendship, then you'll know what you want."

"Good idea. But Seth's three thousand miles away, in case you'd forgotten, and forming a relationship thousands of miles apart isn't going to be easy."

"How did you ever make the dean's list, girl?" Ashley questioned in a scathing tone. "Ever hear of letters? Some people have been known to faithfully deliver those white envelopes and fill their appointed rounds—through snow, through rain—"

"I get the picture," Claudia interrupted.

She had thought about writing Seth, but didn't know his address and didn't know what she could say. One thing she was certain, the next move must come from her. Seth was a proud man. He had made his position clear. The next move was hers.

Ashley left for work a few minutes later, and Claudia mentally toyed with the idea of writing Seth. She didn't need to say anything about his proposal. As usual, her level-headed friend had put things into perspective. Ashley was right. She couldn't make such a major decision without there being more of a basis for their relationship than six days. They could write, phone and even visit each other until Claudia was sure of her feelings. And most of all, she recognized that she couldn't go on living like this.

The letter wasn't easy. Crumbled pieces of paper littered the living room floor. When it got to the point that the carpet had all but disappeared under discarded sheets, Claudia paused and decided it would go better if she ate something. She stood, stretched and was making herself a sandwich when she realized that, for the first time since Seth left, she was actually hungry. A pleased smile spread slowly across her face.

Once she'd eaten, the letter flowed smoothly. She wrote about the weather and her classes, a couple of idiosyncrasies of her professors. She asked him questions about Nome and his business. Finally there were two sheets of neat, orderly handwriting, and she signed it simply: Claudia. Reading it over, she realized so much had been left unsaid. Chewing on the end of her pen, she scribbled in a postscript that said she missed him. Would he understand?

The letter was almost memorized by the time she

dropped it into the mailbox an hour later. Purposely she walked it there, afraid she'd change her mind if the letter lay around all weekend. Because she had no address, she wrote his name and Nome, Alaska. If it arrived, then it would be God's doing. This whole relationship was God's doing.

Calculating roughly that the letter would arrive on Wednesday or Thursday, she guessed that, if he wrote back right away, she could have something from him by the following week. That night she crawled into bed and, for the first time in two and a half desolate weeks, slept peacefully.

All day Thursday, Claudia was fidgety. Seth would get her letter today. How would he react to it? Would he be glad, or had he given up on her completely? How much longer would it be before she knew? How long would it be before she could expect an answer? She smiled as she let herself into the apartment; it was as if she expected something monumental to happen. By ten she'd finished her studies, and after a leisurely bath she read her Bible and went to bed, unreasonably disappointed.

Nothing happened Friday, either. Steve Kali, another medical student, asked her out for coffee after their last lab class and Claudia accepted, pleased at the invitation. Steve was nice. He wasn't Seth, but he was nice.

The phone rang Saturday afternoon. Claudia was bringing in the groceries and dropped a bag of oranges as she rushed across the carpet to answer it.

"Hello." She sounded out of breath.

"Hello, Red," Seth's deep, rich voice returned.

Claudia's hand tightened on the receiver and her

heartbeat accelerated wildly. "You got my letter?" Her voice remained breathless, but it had nothing to do with hurrying to answer the phone.

"About time. I didn't know if I'd ever hear from you," he admonished gently.

Claudia suddenly felt so weak that she sat on a chair. "How are you?"

"Miserable," he admitted harshly. "Your letter sounded so bright and newsy. If you hadn't added that note on the bottom, I don't know what I would have thought."

"Oh, Seth," she breathed into the phone. "I've been wretched. I really do miss you."

"It's about time you admitted as much. I had no idea it would take you this long to realize I was right. Do you want me to fly down there? Alaska requires blood tests."

"Blood tests?"

"Yes, silly woman, they're required for a marriage license."

Chapter Five

"Marriage license? I didn't write because I was ready to change my mind," she denied. Did Seth believe this separation was a battle of wills and she was the first to surrender? "I'm staying here in Seattle, I thought you understood that."

Her announcement was followed by a lengthy pause. Claudia could hear Seth's anger, and the effort he made to control his breathing. "Then why did you write the letter?"

"You still don't understand, do you?" She threw the words at him. "Someday, Seth Lessinger, I'm going to be a fabulous doctor. This has been my dream from the time I was a little girl." She took a calming breath; she didn't want to argue with him.

"Seth, I wrote you because I've been miserable. I've missed you more than I believed possible. I thought it might work if you and I got to know one another better. We can write and—"

"I'm not interested in a pen pal." His laugh was harsh and bitter.

"Neither am I," she returned sharply. "You're being unfair again. Can't we compromise? Do we have to do everything your way? Give me time, that's all I'm asking."

Her words were met with another long silence, and for an apprehensive second Claudia thought he might have hung up on her. "Seth," she whispered, "give me more time, is that so unreasonable?"

"All right, Red, we'll do this your way," he conceded. "But I'm not much for letter writing, and this is a busy time of the year for me, so don't expect much."

Claudia breathed in happily. "I won't." It was a beginning.

Seth's first letter arrived four days later. Home from her classes before Ashley, Claudia stopped to pick up the mail in the apartment vestibule. There was only one letter, with large, bold handwriting. Claudia stared at it with the instant knowledge it was from Seth. Clutching the envelope tightly, she rushed up the stairs, fumbled with the apartment lock and barged in the front door. She tossed her coat and books haphazardly on the couch before tearing open the letter. His, too, was newsy, full of tidbits of information about his job and what this new contract would do for his business, Arctic Barge Company. He told a little about the city of Nome and about what she should expect when she came.

Claudia couldn't prevent the smile that trembled across her lips. When she came, indeed! He also explained that when she packed her things she'd have to ship everything she couldn't bring in her suitcases. Arrangements would need to be made to have her belongings transported on a barge headed North. The only way into Nome was either by air or by sea, and access by sea was limited to a few short weeks in the summer before the water froze again. The pressure for her to make her decision soon was subtle. He concluded by saying that he missed her and, just in case she'd forgotten, he loved her. She read the words and closed her eyes to the flood of emotions that swirled about her.

She answered the letter that night and sent off another two days later. A week passed, and Claudia received another long response from Seth, with an added postscript that there was a possibility he would be in Seattle at the end of October for two days of meetings. He didn't know how much unscheduled time he'd have, but he was hoping to come a day early. Then would be the time for them to sit down and talk, because letters only made him miss her more. He gave her the dates and promised he'd contact her when he knew more. Again he told her he loved her and needed her.

Claudia savored each letter, reading them so many times she knew each one by heart. In some ways, corresponding was building a more solid relationship than having him in Seattle. If he'd been here, Claudia would have been more easily swayed by her physical response to him. This way she could carefully weigh each aspect of her decision and give Seth and the move to Nome prayerful consideration. And she did pray, fervently, every day. But after so many weeks she was beginning to believe God wasn't ever going to answer.

Ashley saw her reading over one of Seth's letters for the tenth time and laughingly threw a decorator pillow at her.

"Hey," Claudia snapped, "what did you do that for?"

"Because I couldn't stand to see you look so miserable!"

"I'm not miserable," Claudia denied. "I'm happy. There's another letter from Seth and . . . and he told me again how much he wants me to marry him and . . ." Her voice cracked and she swallowed back tears that burned for release. "I . . . didn't know I would cry about it."

"You still don't know what you want, do you?"

Claudia shook her head. "I pray and pray and pray, and God doesn't seem to hear me. He gave Seth a sign, but there's nothing for me. It's unfair!"

"What kind of confirmation are you looking for?" Ashley sat beside Claudia and handed her a tissue.

Claudia sniffled and waved her hand dramatically. "I don't know. Just something, anything! When I made my commitment to Christ, I told Him my life was no longer my own but His. If He wants me digging ditches, then I'd dig ditches. If He wants me to give up medical school and marry Seth, then I'd do so in a minute. Seth seems so positive, and I'm so unsure."

Ashley pinched her lips together for a moment, and went into her bedroom, returning a minute later with her Bible. "Do you remember the story of Elijah?"

"I think so. Wasn't he an Old Testament prophet?"

Ashley nodded as she flipped through the worn pages of her Bible. "As I recall, Elijah was hiding from the wicked Jezebel. God sent the angel of the Lord, who led Elijah into a cave. He told him to stay there and wait, because God was coming to speak to him. Elijah waited and waited. When a strong wind came, he rushed from the cave and cried out, but the wind wasn't God. An earthquake followed, and again Elijah hurried outside, certain this time that the earthquake was God speaking to him. But it wasn't the earthquake. Next came a fire, and again Elijah was positive that the fire was God speaking to him. But it wasn't. Finally, when everything was quiet, Elijah heard a soft, gentle whisper. That was the Lord." Ashley transferred the open Bible to Claudia's lap. "Here, read the story yourself."

Thoughtfully Claudia read over the chapter before looking up. "You're telling me I should stop looking for that bolt of lightning in the sky that spells out: *Marry Seth.*"

"Or the handwriting on the wall," Ashley added with a laugh.

"God is answering my prayers—all I need to do is listen?"

"I think so."

"It sounds too simple," Claudia said with a sigh.

"I don't know that it is. But you've got to quit looking for the strong wind, the earthquake and the fire and listen instead to your heart."

"I'm not even positively sure I love him." The magnetic physical attraction between them was overwhelming, but there was so much more to love and a lifetime commitment.

"You'll know," Ashley assured her confidently. "I

don't doubt that for a second. When the timing is right, you'll know."

Claudia felt as if a weight had been lifted from her, and she sighed deeply before forcefully expelling her breath. "Hey, do you know what today is?" she asked, then answered before Ashley had the opportunity, "Columbus Day. A day worthy enough to celebrate with something special." Carefully she tucked Seth's letter back inside the envelope. "Let's bring home Chinese food and drown our doubts in pork fried rice."

"And egg rolls," Ashley added. "Lots of egg rolls."

By the time they returned to the apartment, Claudia and Ashley had collected more than dinner. Claudia met Steve Kali and a friend of his at the restaurant, and after quick introductions, the four decided they could get two extra items off the menu if they ordered together.

They sat on the floor in a large circle at Ashley and Claudia's apartment, eating their meal with chopsticks out of the white carry-out boxes. Everything was passed around the circle.

Steve's friend, Dave Kimball, was a law student who immediately showed a keen interest in Ashley. Claudia watched with an amused smile as Ashley responded with some flirtations of her own.

The chopsticks were soon abandoned in favor of more common utensils, but the laughter continued.

"You know what we're celebrating, don't you?" Ashley questioned between bites of ginger-spiced beef and tomato.

"No." Both men shook their heads, glancing from one girl to the other.

"Columbus Day," Claudia supplied.

" 'Columbus sailed the ocean blue'?" Steve jumped up and danced around the room singing.

Everyone laughed.

The phone rang and Steve picked up the receiver. "I'll answer that," he volunteered, "it might be a phone call." He promptly dropped the phone. "Oops, sorry," he apologized into the receiver.

Claudia couldn't help smiling. Steve didn't mean to be flip, he was just having a good time. She was, too; it felt good to laugh again. Ashley was right, this whole thing with Seth was too intense. She needed to relax. Her decision must be based on the quiet knowledge that marriage to Seth was what God had ordained.

"I'm sorry, would you mind repeating that?" Steve said into the earpiece. "Claudia? Yeah, she's here." He covered the receiver with the palm of his hand. "Are you here, Claudia?" he asked with a satisfied smirk.

"You nut. Give me that." She stood and took the phone. "Hello." Just her luck, it'd be Cooper, who'd demand to know what a man was doing in her apartment. "This is Claudia."

"What's going on?"

The color drained out of her flushed cheeks. "Seth?" she asked incredulously. Breathlessly, she repeated herself. "Seth, it is really you?"

"It's me," he confirmed, his tone brittle. "Who's the guy who answered the phone."

"Oh." She swallowed, and turned her back to the others. "That's Steve Kali, a friend of mine from school. There are several friends here," she explained, stretching the truth. She didn't want Seth to get the wrong impression. "We're celebrating Columbus Day . . . you know, Columbus, the man who sailed the three ships across the blue Atlantic looking for India and discovered America instead. Do you celebrate that day in Alaska?" She continued to babble.

"I know what day it is. You sound like you've been drinking."

"Not unless the Chinese tea's got something in it I don't know about."

"Who's the guy who answered the phone?"

The last thing Claudia wanted to do was make explanations to Seth with everyone listening to the conversation. There'd never been any need for more than one phone before. "It really would be better if we talked later," she said, stammering slightly.

"Everyone's there listening, right?" Seth guessed.

"Right," she confirmed on a soft sigh. "Do you mind?"

"No, but before you hang up, answer me one thing. Have you been thinking about how much I love you and want you here with me?"

"Oh, Seth," she murmured miserably. "Yes, I've thought of little else."

"And you still don't know?" he asked, his voice heavy with exasperation.

"Not yet."

"All right, Red. I'll call back in an hour."

Actually, it was almost two hours before the phone rang again. Steve and Dave had left an hour before, and Ashley had made a flimsy excuse about needing to do some research work at the library. Claudia didn't question her and appreciated the privacy.

She answered the phone on the first ring. "Hello."

"Now tell me who the guy was who picked up the phone the first time," Seth demanded.

Claudia's light laugh drifted pleasantly into the receiver. "Seth Lessinger, you sound almost jealous."

"Almost?" he shouted back.

"His name's Steve Kali, we have several classes together, that's all," she explained, pleased at his small display of concern. "I didn't know you were the jealous sort," she admonished gently.

"I never have been before. I don't like the way it feels either, if that makes you any happier."

"I'd feel the same way," she admitted. "I wish you were here, Seth. Ashley and I walked by a skating rink tonight and stopped to watch some couples skating together. Do you realize that you and I have never skated? If I close my eyes, I can almost feel your arm around me."

Seth sucked in his breath. "Why do you say things like that when we're separated by thousands of miles? Your sense of timing is sadly misplaced. Besides, we don't need skating as an excuse for me to be near you," he murmured, his voice disturbed and low. "Listen, honey, I'll be in Seattle a week from Saturday."

"Saturday? Oh, Seth!" She was too happy to express her thoughts. "It'll be so good to see you!"

"My plane arrives early that morning. I'll phone you as soon as I can review the conference schedule."

"I won't plan a thing. No," she said, laughing, "I'll plan everything. Can you stay over until Monday? I'll skip classes and we could have a whole extra day alone."

"I can't." He sounded as disappointed as she.

They talked for an hour, and Claudia felt guilty at the thought of his phone bill, but the conversation had been wonderful.

Did she love him? The question kept repeating itself all the next week. If she could truthfully answer that one question, then the other would answer itself. Just talking to him over the phone had lifted her spirits dramatically. But could she leave school and everything, everyone, she had ever known and follow him to a harsh, cruel land?

Her last class Friday of the following week was a disaster. Her attention span was no longer than a four-year-old's. Time and time again she was forced to bring herself back into reality. So many conflicting emotions seemed to be coming at her. The first big tests of the quarter, Seth's visit. She felt pounded and burdened from every side, tormented by her own indecision.

Steve walked out of the building with her.

"Why so glum?" he asked. "If anyone's got complaints, it should be me." They continued down the stairs, and Claudia cast him a sidelong glance.

"What have you got to complain about?"

"Plenty," he began in an irritated tone. "You remember Dave Kimball?"

Claudia nodded, recalling Steve's tall, sandy-haired friend who had flirted so outrageously with Ashley. "Sure, I remember Dave."

"We got picked up by the police a couple of nights ago."

Claudia glanced apprehensively at her friend. "What happened?"

"Nothing, really. We'd both been having a good time and decided to walk home after several beers.

About halfway to the dorm, Dave starts with the crazies. He was climbing up the streetlights, jumping on parked cars. I wasn't doing any of this, but we were both brought into the police station for disorderly conduct."

Claudia's blue eyes rounded incredulously. Steve was one of the straightest, most clean-cut men she had met. This was so unlike anything she'd suspect from him, she didn't know how to react.

"That's not the half of it," Steve continued. "Once we were at the police station, Dave kept insisting that he was a law student and knew his rights. He demanded his one phone call."

"Well, it's probably a good thing he did know what to do," Claudia said.

"Dave made his one call all right." Steve inhaled a shaky breath. "And twenty minutes later the desk sergeant came in to ask which one of us ordered the pizza."

Claudia burst into giggles, but it wasn't long before Steve joined her. He placed a friendly arm around her shoulders as their laughter faded. Together they strolled toward the parking lot.

"I do feel bad about the police thing. . . ." Before she could complete her thought, she caught sight of a broad-shouldered man walking toward her with crisp strides. She knew immediately it was Seth.

His look of contempt was aimed directly at her, his rough features darkened by a fierce frown. Even from the narrowing distance, she recognized the tight set of his mouth as he glared at her.

Steve's arm resting lightly across her shoulders felt as if it weighed a thousand pounds.

Chapter Six

Claudia's mouth became dry as she quickened her pace and rushed forward to meet Seth. If his look hadn't been so angry and forbidding, she would have walked directly into his arms. "When—how did you get here? I thought you couldn't come until tomorrow?" Only now was she recovering from the shock of seeing him.

An unwilling smile broke his stern expression as he pulled her to him and crushed her in his embrace.

Half lifted from the sidewalk, Claudia linked her hands behind his neck and felt his warm breath in her hair. "Oh, Seth," she mumbled, close to tears, "you idiot, why didn't you say something?"

So many emotions came at her at once. She felt crushed yet protected, jubilant yet tearful, excited but afraid. To each sensation she responded with equal fervor by spreading eager kisses over his face.

Slowly he released her and the two men eyed each other skeptically.

Seth extended his hand. "I'm Seth Lessinger, Claudia's fiancé."

Claudia had to bite into her lip to keep from correcting him, but she wouldn't say anything that could destroy this minute.

Steve's eyes rounded with immediate surprise, but he managed to mumble a greeting and exchange handshakes. He made some excuse about catching the bus and was gone.

"Who's that?"

"Steve," she replied, too happy to see him to question the way he had introduced himself to her fellow student. "He answered the phone the other night when you called. He's just a friend, don't worry."

"Then why did he have his arm around you?" Seth demanded with growing impatience.

Claudia ignored the question, instead standing on the tips of her toes and lightly brushing her mouth over his. His whiskers tickled her face, and she lifted both hands to his dark beard, framing his lips so she could kiss him soundly.

Seth's response was immediate as he pulled her into his arms. "I've missed you. I won't be able to wait much longer. Who would believe this little slip of nothing could bring this giant to his knees? Literally," he added.

Claudia's eyes widened with feigned offense. "Little slip of nothing? Come now, you make me sound like a young Shirley Temple!"

He laughed; it was the robust, deep laugh that she loved. "Compared to me, you're pint-size." Looping his arm around her waist, he walked beside her. Again Claudia felt cradled and loved beyond anything she had known. She smiled up at him, and his eyes drank deeply from hers as a slow grin spread over his face, crinkling tiny lines at his eyes. "You may be small, but you hold powers over me I don't think I'll ever understand."

Leaning her head against the crook of his arm, Claudia relaxed. "Why didn't you say anything about coming today?"

"I didn't know that I was going to make the flight until the last minute. As it was, I hired a pilot out of Nome to make the connection with Alaska Airlines in Fairbanks."

"How'd you know where to find me?"

"I met Ashley at your apartment. She drew me a map of the campus and told me where you'd be. You don't mind?"

"Of course not," she assured him with a smile and a shake of her head. "I just wish I'd known. I could have met you at the airport."

She gave him her car keys and he drove the silver compact, but it wasn't until they were in heavy afternoon traffic that she noticed Seth was heading in the opposite direction from her apartment.

"Where are we going?" She looked down at her navy-blue cords and Irish cable-knit sweater. She wasn't dressed for anything but a casual outing.

"My hotel," he answered without looking at her, focusing his attention on the freeway. "I wanted to talk to you privately, and from the look of things at your place, Ashley is going to be around for a while."

Ashley was involved in a project that she'd been working on for two nights. Magazines, newspapers and several loose sheets of written notes were scattered over the living room floor.

"I know what you mean about the apartment." She laughed softly in understanding. Most likely Ashley had been engrossed in it all when Seth arrived. "Did you get a chance to talk to my roommate?"

"Not too much." He slowed the car as he pulled off the freeway and onto Mercer Avenue. "She's a nice girl. I like her. Those blue eyes are almost as beautiful as yours."

Something twitched in Claudia's stomach. Jealousy —over Ashley? She was her best friend! Quickly she tossed the thought aside.

Seth's hand reached for hers. Linking their fingers, he carried her hand to his mouth and gently kissed her knuckles. Shivers tingled up her arm and she smiled contentedly.

The downtown hotel lobby was bristling with activity. Suitcases littered the richly carpeted floor, while the continuous ringing of bells alerted the bellhops to where they were needed. In contrast, Seth's room was quiet and serene. Situated high above the city, the large suite displayed a sweeping view of Puget Sound and the landmarks Seattle was famous for: the Pacific Science Center, the Space Needle and the Kingdome.

The king-size bed was bordered on each side by oak nightstands with white ceramic lamps. Two easy chairs were set obliquely in front of a color television. Claudia glanced uneasily over the room, feeling slightly uncomfortable.

The door had no sooner closed when Seth placed a hand on her shoulder and turned her around to face him. Their eyes met, hers uncertain and a little afraid, his warm and reassuring. When he slipped his arms around her, she came willingly, fitting herself against the hard contours of his solid length. Relaxing, she savored the fiery warmth of his kiss. She slipped her hands behind his neck and yielded with the knowledge that she wanted him to kiss her, needed his kisses. Nothing on earth had been so close to heaven than being cradled in his arms.

Arms of corded steel locked her, held her close. Yet he was gentle, as if she was the most precious thing in the world. With a muted groan, he dragged his mouth from hers and showered the side of her neck with urgent kisses.

"I shouldn't be doing this," he moaned hoarsely. "But I don't know if I have the will to stop." One hand continued down her back, arching her upward while the fingers of the other hand played havoc with her hair.

Claudia's mind was caught in a whirl of desire and need. This shouldn't be happening, but it felt so right. For a moment she wanted to question him. They should wait until they were married. But she couldn't speak. Seth pulled away and paused, his eyes searching hers. His breath came in uneven gasps.

This was the time to stop, to back away, but she couldn't. The long weeks of separation, the doubts, the uncertainties that had plagued her night and day, the restless dreams all exploded in her mind as she lifted her arms to him. It had been like this between them almost from the beginning, this magnetic, overpowering attraction.

Seth released a shuddering sigh as he slipped a hand under her sweater. His hands roved the soft skin of her bare back, soothing and caressing.

A rush of cold air hit her and Claudia inhaled a slow breath. She closed her eyes, suddenly frightened by the hungry look in his eyes.

Slowly Seth lowered his mouth to hers until their breaths merged, and the kiss that followed sent her world in a crazy spin.

"I can't do it." The bitter words were whispered hoarsely in her ear, barely distinct. "I can't," he repeated and broke the embrace.

The words flittered through her consciousness and Claudia forced her eyes open. Seth was standing away from her. He wasn't smiling now, and the troubled, almost tormented expression puzzled her all the more.

"Seth," she whispered, "what is it?"

"I'm sorry." He crossed his arms and turned his back, as if offering her the chance to escape.

Her arms felt as if they'd been weighed down with lead, and her heart felt numb, as if she'd been exposed to the Arctic cold without the proper protective gear.

"Forgive me, Red." Seth covered his eyes with a weary hand and walked across the room to stand before the window. "I brought you here with the worst of intentions," he began. "I thought if we were to make love, then all your doubts would be gone." He paused to take in a labored breath. "I knew you'd marry me then without question."

Understanding burned like a laser beam searing through her mind, and she half moaned, half cried. Her arms cradled her stomach as the pain washed over her. Color blazed in her cheeks at how close she had come to letting their passion rage out of control. It had been a trick, a farce, in order for Seth to exert his will over her.

Several minutes passed in silence. Claudia turned to Seth, his profile was outlined by the dim light of dusk. He seemed to be struggling for control of his emotions.

"I wouldn't blame you if you hated me after this," he spoke at last.

"I . . . I don't hate you." Her voice was unsteady, soft and trembling.

"You don't love me either, do you?" He hurled the words at her accusingly and turned to face her.

The muscles in her throat constricted painfully. "I don't know. I just don't know."

"Will you ever be completely sure?" he questioned her with thinning patience.

Claudia buried her face in her hands, defeated and miserable.

"Red, please don't cry. I'm sorry." The anger was gone and he spoke softly, reassuringly.

She shivered with reaction. "If . . . if we did get married, could I stay here until I finished my schooling?"

"No," he returned adamantly. "I want a wife and children. Look at me, Red. I'm thirty-six; I can't wait another five, six years for a family. And I work too hard to divide my life between Nome and Seattle."

Wasn't there any compromise? Did everything have to be his way? "You're asking for so much," she cried.

"But I'm offering even more," he countered.

"You don't understand," she told him. "If I give up school now, I'll probably never be able to finish.

Especially if I won't be able to come back for several years."

"There isn't any compromise," he said with a note of finality. "If God wants you to be a doctor, He'll provide the way later. We both have to trust Him for that."

"I can't give it all up. It's not that easy," she whispered.

"Then there's nothing left to say, is there?" Dark shadows of doubt clouded his face, and he turned sharply and resumed his position in front of the window.

There didn't seem to be anything left to do but to leave quietly. She forced herself to open the door, but knew she couldn't let it end like this. Softly the door clicked shut.

At the sound Seth slammed his fist against the window ledge. Claudia gave a small cry of alarm and he pivoted to face her. His rugged features were contorted with anger as he stared at her. But one look told Claudia the anger was directed at himself and not her.

"I thought you'd gone." His gaze held hers.

"I couldn't," she whispered.

He stared deeply into her liquid blue eyes and paused as if he wanted to say something, but instead shook his head in defeat.

Claudia's eyes were red and haunted as she covered the distance between them. She slid her hands around his waist, hugging him while she rested a tearstained cheek against his back.

"We have something very special, Red, but it's not going to work." The dejected tone of his voice stabbed at her heart.

"It'll work. I know it will. Everything's my fault, I know that. But I want to be sure, very sure, before I make such a drastic change in my life. Give me time, that's all I'm asking."

"You've had almost six weeks."

"It's not enough."

He tried to remove her hands, but she squeezed all the tighter. "We're both hurt and angry tonight, but that doesn't mean things between us won't work."

"I could almost believe you," Seth murmured and altered their position so that she was securely wrapped in his arms.

She met his penetrating gaze and answered in a soft, throbbing voice, "Believe me, Seth. Please believe me."

His gaze slid to her lips before his mouth claimed hers in a fierce and flaming kiss that was almost savage, as if to punish her for the torment she had caused him. But it didn't matter how he kissed her as long as she hadn't lost him.

They had dinner at the hotel, but didn't return to Seth's room. They discussed his conference schedule, which included several meetings the following day. His plane left early Sunday afternoon. They made plans for Seth to attend the Sunday morning church service with Claudia and for her to drive him to the airport afterward.

Claudia's heart was heavy all the next day. Several times she wished she could talk to Seth, clear away the ghosts of yesterday. For those long, miserable weeks she had missed him so much that she could hardly function. Then at the first chance to see each other again, they had ended up fighting. Why didn't she know what to do? Was this torment her heart suffered love?

The question remained unanswered as they sat together in church Sunday morning. It felt so right to have Seth by her side. Claudia closed her eyes to pray, fervently asking God to guide her. She paused, recalling the verses she had found in the Gospel of Matthew about asking, seeking, knocking. God had promised that anyone who asks receives, and anyone who seeks finds. It had all sounded so simple and straightforward when she read it, but it wasn't—not for her.

When she finished her prayer and opened her eyes, she felt Seth's gaze burn over her, searching her face. She longed to reassure him, but could find no words. Gently she reached for his hand and squeezed it.

They rode to the airport in an uneasy silence. Their time had been wasted for the most part. What Claudia had hoped would be a time to settle doubts had only raised more.

"You don't need to come inside with me," Seth said as they neared the airport. His words sliced into her troubled thoughts.

"What?" she asked, confused and hurt. "But I want to be with you as long as possible."

He didn't look pleased with her decision. "Fine, if that's what you want."

The set of his mouth was angry and impatient, but Claudia didn't know why. "You don't want me there, do you?" She tried to hide the hurt in her voice.

His cool eyes met her look of defiance. "Oh, for goodness' sake, settle down, Red. I take it all back. Come in if you want. I didn't mean to make a federal case out of this." The appeasement was issued in a rumbling tone.

Claudia didn't want to argue again, not in their last minutes together. Seth continued to look withdrawn. They parked in the cement garage and walked into the main terminal to check his luggage.

Tentatively her hand reached out to rest on his arm. "Friends?" she asked and offered him a smile.

He returned the gesture and tenderly squeezed her delicate hand. "Friends."

The thick atmosphere melted and the tension eased as she waited while Seth reported to the airline desk with his ticket and suitcases. He returned with a wry grin.

"The flight's been delayed an hour. How about some lunch?"

Claudia couldn't prevent the smile that softly curved her mouth. Her eyes reflected her pleasure at the unexpected time together.

They ate at an airport restaurant, but Claudia noted that Seth barely touched his meal. Her appetite wasn't up to par, either. Another separation loomed before them.

"How long will it be before you'll be back?" Claudia asked as they walked toward the departure gate.

There was a moment of grim hesitation before Seth answered. "I don't know. Months probably. This conference wasn't necessary. If it hadn't been for you, I wouldn't have attended. I can't afford to take time away from my business like this."

Claudia swallowed at the lump forming in her throat. "Thanksgiving break is coming soon. Maybe I could fly up and visit you. I'd like to see for myself the beauty of Alaska. You've told me so much about it already." Just for a moment, for a fleeting second, she was tempted to drop everything and leave with him now. Quickly she buried the impulsive thought and clenched her fists together inside the pockets of her wool coat.

Seth didn't respond either way to her suggestion that she come and visit him.

"What do you think?" she prompted.

Seth inclined his head and nodded faintly. "If that's what you'd like."

Claudia had the feeling he hadn't understood any of what she'd been saying.

When the time came for him to board the plane, her façade of composure began to slip. It was difficult to restrain her tears, and she blinked several times, not wanting Seth to remember her with tears shimmering in her eyes. With a proud lift of her chin she offered him a brave smile.

He studied her unhappy face. "Good-bye, Red." His eyes continued to hold hers.

The hesitation before her answer emphasized all the more her inner turmoil. "Good-bye, Seth," she whispered softly, a slight catch to her voice.

The palm of his hand cupped her face and his thumb gently wiped away a single tear that was weaving a slow course down her pale face. Claudia buried her chin in his hand and gently kissed the calloused palm.

Gathering her into his embrace, Seth wrapped his arms around her as he buried his face in her neck and breathed in deeply. When his mouth found hers, the kiss was gentle and sweet and so full of love that fresh tears misted her eyes. She sniffed to abate their fall.

His hold relaxed and he began to pull away, but she wouldn't let him. "Seth." She murmured his name urgently. She had meant to let him go, relinquish him without a word, but somehow she couldn't.

He scooped her in his arms, crushing her against him with a fierceness that stole her breath away. "I'm a man," he bit out in an impatient tremor, "and I can't take much more of this." He released her enough to study her face. His dark eyes clearly revealed his needs. "I'm asking you again, Claudia. Marry me and come to Nome. I promise you a good life. I need you."

Claudia felt raw. The soft, womanly core of her cried out a resounding yes, but the decision would be based on the emotion of the moment. She didn't want to decide something so important to both of them on the basis of feelings. Indecision and uncertainty raced through her mind, and she could neither deny nor accept him. Unable to formulate words, she found a low, protesting groan slipping from her throat. Her brimming blue eyes pleaded with him for understanding.

Seth's gaze sliced into her as a hardness stole into his features, narrowing his mouth. Forcefully he turned and with quick, impatient steps made for the plane.

Unable to do anything more, Claudia watched him enter the jetway. Still crushed by her emotions, she stood by the large windows waiting until the plane was in the sky.

The following week was wretched. At times Claudia thought it would have been easier not to have seen Seth again than endure the misery of another parting. To complicate her life further, it was the week of midterm exams. Never had she felt less like studying. Each night she wrote Seth long, flowing letters. School had always come first, but suddenly writing letters to Seth was more important. When she did study, her concentration waned and her mind wandered to the hurt look on Seth's face before he'd entered the plane. The look haunted her all week. She did poorly on the first test, her drive to excel weakening to lack of interest. Determined to do better on the next series of exams, Claudia forced herself to study. The textbooks lay open on top of the kitchen table, and Claudia's chin was propped on both hands as she stared into space. Her thoughts weren't on school but on Seth. The illogical meanderings of her mind continued to haunt her with the burning question of her future. Was being a pediatrician so important if it meant loosing Seth?

"You look like a lovesick calf," Ashley commented as she strolled into the kitchen to pour herself a glass of milk.

"I feel like one," Claudia returned miserably.

"There's something different about you since Seth's gone back to Alaska."

"No there isn't," she denied. "It's all the hassles of these tests." Why did she feel the need to make excuses? She'd always been able to talk to Ashley about anything.

Her roommate gave her a funny look, but didn't say anything. A minute later she returned to the living room.

Angry with herself and the world, Claudia studied half the night, finally staggering into her bedroom at about three. That was another thing. She hadn't been sleeping well since Seth had gone.

Ashley was cooking dinner when Claudia arrived

home the next afternoon. She'd gone to the library, hoping to keep her mind off Seth and concentrate on her schoolwork.

"You had company," Ashley announced casually, but she looked a bit flushed and slightly uneasy.

Claudia's heart stopped. Seth. Seth had come back for her. She needed so desperately to see him again, to talk to him.

"Seth?" she questioned breathlessly.

"No, Cooper. I didn't know what time you were going to be home, so instead of waiting here, he decided to run an errand and come back later," Ashley explained.

"Oh." Claudia didn't even try to disguise the disappointment in her voice. "I can do without another unpleasant confrontation with my uncle. I wonder how he found out about that awful test grade so early."

"Why do you always assume the worse with Cooper?" Ashley demanded with a sharp edge of impatience. "I, for one, happen to think he's nice. I don't think I've ever seen him treat anyone unfairly. It seems to me that you're the one who—" She stopped abruptly and turned back toward the stove, stirring the frying hamburger with unnecessary vigor. "I hope spaghetti sounds good."

"Sure," Claudia responded. "Anything."

Cooper didn't arrive until they had eaten and were clearing off the table. Claudia made a pot of coffee and brought him a cup in the living room. She could feel his gaze studying her.

"You don't look so good," he commented, taking the cup and saucer out of her hand. Most men would have preferred a mug, but not Cooper.

"So Ashley keeps telling me." She sat opposite him. "Don't do the dishes, Ash," she called into the kitchen. "Wait until later and I'll help."

"No need." Ashley stuck her head around the kitchen door. "You go ahead and visit. Call if you need anything."

"No, Ashley," Cooper stood as he spoke. "I think that it might be beneficial if you were here, too."

Ashley looked from one to the other, dried her hands on a towel and came into the room.

"I don't mean to embarrass you, Ashley, but in all fairness I think Claudia should know that you were the one to contact me."

Claudia's gaze shot accusingly across the room. "What do you mean?"

Ashley shrugged. "I've been so worried about you lately. You're hardly yourself anymore. I thought if you talked to Cooper, it might help you make up your mind. You can't go on like this, Claudia." Her voice was gentle and stern all at the same time.

"What do you mean?" She vaulted to her feet. "This is unfair, both of you against me."

"Against you?" Cooper echoed. "Come now, Claudia, you seem to have misjudged everything."

"No I haven't." Tears threatened her eyes, burning for release.

"I think it would probably be best if I left the two of you alone." Ashley stood and excused herself, returning to the kitchen.

Claudia hurled her an angry glare as she stepped past. Some friend!

"I hope you'll talk honestly with me, Claudia," Cooper began. "I'd like to know what's got you so upset that you're a stranger to your own best friend."

"Nothing," she denied adamantly, but her voice cracked and the first tears began spilling down her cheek.

Claudia was sure Cooper had never seen her cry. He looked at a loss as he stood and searched hurriedly through his suit coat for a handkerchief. Just watching him made Claudia want to laugh, and she hiccuped in an attempt to restrain tears and laughter.

"Here." He handed her a white linen cloth, crisply pressed. Claudia didn't care, she wiped her eyes and blew her nose. "I'm fine, really," she declared in a wavering voice.

"It's about Seth, isn't it?" Cooper prompted.

She nodded, blowing her nose again. "He wants me to marry him and move to Alaska."

The room suddenly became still as Cooper digested the information. "Are you going to do it?" he asked in a quiet voice she had long ago learned to decipher as a warning.

"If I knew that, I wouldn't be here blubbering like an idiot," she returned defensively.

"I can't help but believe it would be a mistake," Cooper continued. "Lessinger's a good man, don't misunderstand me, but I don't think you'd be happy in Alaska. Where did you say he was from again?" he asked.

"Nome."

"I don't suppose there's a university in Nome for you to continue your studies?"

"No." The word was clipped, impatient.

Cooper nodded. "You were meant to be a doctor," he said confidently as he rose to his feet. "You'll get over Seth. There's probably a fine young man you'll meet later."

"Sure," she agreed without enthusiasm.

Cooper left a few minutes later, and at the sound of the door closing, Ashley stepped out of the kitchen. "You aren't mad, are you?"

At first Claudia had been, but not now. At least she knew where Cooper stood on the subject and what she would face if she did decide to marry Seth.

"Oh, Seth," she whispered that night, sitting up in bed. He hadn't contacted her since his return, not even answering her long letters. Eagerly Claudia had checked the mail every day. After several days she understood that the next move would have to be from her. Her Bible rested on her knees, and she opened it for her devotional reading in Hebrews. She read Chapter 11 twice, the famous chapter on faith. Had Rebekah acted in faith when the servant had come to her family, claiming God had given him a sign? Flipping through the pages of her Bible, she turned to Genesis to reread the story Seth had quoted. When Seth had given her the engagement ring they had argued. Claudia had said Rebekah probably didn't have any choice in the matter, but reading the story now, Claudia noted that the Bible said she did. Rebekah's family asked her if she was willing to go with Abraham's servant, and she'd replied that she would.

Rebekah went willingly! Claudia reread the verses again as a sense of release came over her. Her hands trembled with excitement as she closed the Bible and stopped to pray. The prayer was so familiar: asking God's guidance and stating her willingness to do as He wished. But there was a difference this time. The peace she had so desperately sought was there, and she knew that she, too, would answer Seth in faith and respond willingly.

Slipping out of the sheets, she opened the drawer that contained the jeweler's box and the engagement ring. With a contented, happy sigh, she hugged it to her brèast. The temptation was to slip the ring on her finger now. But she'd wait until Seth could do it.

Claudia slept peacefully that night for the first time since Seth had left. She didn't go to classes the next morning.

Ashley looked at her with surprise. Claudia was still in her pajamas when she was dressed and ready to go out the front door. "Did you oversleep? I'm sorry I didn't wake you, but I thought I heard you moving around in your room."

"You did," she answered cheerfully, but her eyes grew serious as her gaze sought Ashley's. "I've decided what to do, Ash," she announced solemnly. "I love Seth. I'm going to him as fast as I can make the arrangements."

Ashley's blue eyes widened with joy as she laughed and hugged her friend. "It's about time. You nut, I knew all along that the two of you belonged together! I'm so happy for you."

Once the decision was made, there seemed to be a hundred things to be dealt with all at once. Claudia phoned Nome almost immediately, her fingers trembling and reached Seth's secretary, who told her Seth had flown to Kotzebue on an emergency. She didn't know when he would be returning, but would give him the message as soon as he walked in the door. Releasing a sigh of disappointment, Claudia replaced the phone in its cradle.

Undaunted by the uncertainties, Claudia drove to

the university and officially withdrew from school. Next she purchased several outfits she would be needing to face an Arctic winter, and a beautiful wedding dress. Lastly she stopped off at Cooper's office.

He smiled broadly when she entered his office. "You look in better spirits today," he greeted. "I knew our little talk would help."

"You'd better sit down, Cooper," she said and smiled. "I've made my decision. I love Seth. I've withdrawn from school and have made arrangements for my things to be shipped North when possible. I'm marrying Seth Lessinger."

Cooper stood, his eyes raking over her. "That's what you think."

Chapter Seven

It was dark and stormy when the plane made a jerky landing on the Nome runway. Claudia shifted to relieve her muscles, tired and stiff from the bouncing ride. The aircraft had hit turbulent weather shortly after takeoff from Anchorage, and the remainder of the flight could be compared to a roller-coaster ride. More than once Claudia had felt the pricklings of fear, but none of the other passengers showed any concern, so she had accepted the jarring ride as a normal part of flying in Alaska.

Her blue eyes glinted with excitement as she stood and gathered the small bag stored in the compartment above the seat. There wasn't a jetway to usher her into a dry, warm airport. When she stepped from the cozy interior of the plane, she was greeted by a solid blast of Arctic wind. The bitter iciness stole her breath, and she groped for the handrail to maintain her balance. Halfway down the stairs, she was nearly ripped away by a fresh gust of wind. Her hair flew into her face, blinding her vision. Unable to move either up or down, she stood stationary until the force of the wind decreased.

Unexpectedly the small bag was wrenched from her numb fingers and she was pulled into the protective hold of a solid form.

He shouted something at her, but the wind carried his voice into the night and there was no distinguishing the message.

Claudia tried to speak, but soon realized the uselessness of talking. She was half carried, half dragged down the remainder of the steps. Once on solid ground, they both struggled against the ferocity of the wind as it whipped and lashed against them. If the man hadn't taken the brunt of the force, Claudia might not have made it inside.

As they came close to the terminal, the door was opened by someone who'd been standing by, watching. The welcoming warmth immediately stirred life into Claudia's frozen body. Nothing could have prepared her for the intensity of the Arctic cold. Even before she could turn and thank her rescuer she was pulled into his arms and crushed in a smothering embrace.

"Seth?" Her arms slid around his thick-coated waist as she returned the urgency of his hug.

He buried his face in her neck and breathed her

name. His hold was punishing, and when he spoke, his voice was tight and worried.

"Are you all right?" Gently his hands framed her face, pushing back the strands of hair that had been whipped across her cheek. His eyes searched her features as if looking for any sign of harm.

"I'm fine," she assured him and, wrapping her arms around him a second time, pressed her face into his coat. "I'm so glad to be here."

"I've been sick with worry," he ground out hoarsely. "The storm hit here several hours ago, and there wasn't any way your flight could avoid the worst of it."

"I'm fine, really." Her voice wobbled, not because she was shaky from the flight, but from the effect of being in Seth's arms.

"I was with the air traffic controller when he first made contact with your pilot and heard the pilot claim that your plane was being batted around like a tennis ball. If anything had happened to you, I don't know . . ." He let the rest fade, and tightened his already secure hold.

"Now that you mention it, I do feel something like a tennis ball," she teased with a happy look and lightly touched her lips to the corner of his mouth.

Seth released her. The worried look in his eyes had diminished now that he knew she was safe. "Let's get out of here," he said abruptly and left her standing alone as he secured her luggage.

The suitcases contained only a small part of her possessions. In the days preceding her flight she'd packed her things and made arrangements to have them shipped to her in the spring. Everything she could possibly get into the three large suitcases would have to see her through until the freight barge arrived.

They rode to the hotel in a four-wheel-drive vehicle. Neither spoke as Seth gave his full attention to manipulating the car through the streets. Claudia looked around her in awe. The barren land was covered with snow. The road was merely compact dirt and snow. The buildings were a dingy gray color. In her dreams she had conjured up romantic pictures of Seth's life in Nome. Reality shattered the vision as the winds buffeted the large car.

The hotel room was neat and clean—not elegant, but she hadn't expected the homey, welcoming appeal. It contained a bed with a plain white bedspread, a small nightstand, a lamp, a telephone and one chair. Seth followed her in, managing the suitcases.

"You packed enough," he said with a sarcastic undertone. Claudia ignored the comment and busied herself by removing her coat to hang it in the bare closet. She gave him a puzzled look. Something was wrong. He had hardly spoken to her since they'd left the airport. At first she'd assumed the tight set of his mouth was a result of the storm, but not now, when she was safe and ready for his love. Her heart ached for him to hold her. Every part of her longed to have him slip the engagement ring onto the third finger of her left hand.

"How's school?" Again the inflection in his voice was derisive.

"Fine."

He remained on the far side of the room, his hands clenched at his sides.

"Let me take your coat?" she offered. As she studied him, the gnawing sensation that something

wasn't right increased. Seth unfastened the coat opening, but he didn't remove his thick parka. He sat at
the end of the bed, his face tight and drawn. Claudia
wasn't sure he'd heard her.

Resting his elbows on his knees, he leaned forward
and buried his face in his hands.

"Seth, what's wrong?" she asked calmly, although
she was far from feeling self-possessed.

"I've only had eight hours' sleep in the last four
days. A tanker caught fire in port at Kotzebue, and
I've been there doing what I could for the past week.
You certainly couldn't have chosen a worse time for a
visit. Isn't it a little early for Thanksgiving?"

Claudia wanted to scream that this wasn't a visit,
she'd come to stay, to be his wife and share his world.
But again she remained quiet, guided by the same
inner sense. Seth's manner, once he'd been assured
she was safe, had been distant, even aloof.

Quietly Seth stood and stalked to the far side of the
small room. He seemed to be limping slightly. He
paused and glanced over his shoulder, but didn't
return to her.

Uncertainty clouded her deep blue eyes and her
mind raced with a thousand questions.

"I'm flying back to Kotzebue as soon as possible. I
shouldn't have taken the time away as it is." He
turned around and his eyes burned her with the
intensity of his glare. His mouth was drawn, hard and
inflexible. "I'll have one of my men drive you back to
the airport for the first available flight to Anchorage."
There was no apology, no explanation, no regrets.

Claudia stared back at him in shocked disbelief.
Even if he had assumed she was here for a short visit,
he was treating her as he would unwanted baggage.

Belying the hurt, she smiled lamely. "I can't see why I have to leave. Even if you aren't here, this would be a good opportunity for me to see Nome. I'd like to—"

"Can't you do as I ask, just once?" he shouted.

She lowered her gaze to fight the anger building within her. Squaring her shoulders, she prepared for the worst. "There's something I don't know, isn't there?" she asked in quiet challenge. She wanted to hear the truth, even at the risk of being hurt.

Her question was followed by a moment of grim silence. "I don't want you here."

"I believe you've made that obvious." Her fingers trembled, and she mentally chided herself for the telltale mannerism.

"I tried to reach you before you left." He gestured defeatedly with his hand.

She didn't comment but continued to stare at him with round, questioning eyes.

"It's not going to work between us, Claudia," he announced solemnly. "I think I realized as much when you didn't return with me when I gave you the ring. You must think I was a fool to propose to you the way I did."

"You know I didn't, I—"

He interrupted her again. "I want a wife, Claudia, not some virtuous doctor out to heal the world. I need a woman, not an insecure, immature little girl who can't decide what she wants in life."

White-lipped, Claudia stiffened her back and met the building rage with feigned control. "Do you want me to hate you, Seth?" she asked softly as her fingers picked an imaginary piece of lint from the sleeve of her thick sweater.

He released a bitter sigh. "Yes. It would make things between us a lot easier if you hated me," he replied flatly. He walked away as if he couldn't bear to see the pain he was causing her. "Even if you were to change your mind and relinquish your lofty dreams to marry me, I doubt that we could make a marriage work. You've been tossing on a wave of indecision for so long, I don't think you'll ever decide what you really want."

Claudia studied the pattern of the worn carpet, biting her tongue to keep from crying out that she knew what she wanted now. But Seth had witnessed her struggle in the sea of uncertainty. He would assume that her decision was as fickle as the turning tide.

"If we married, what's there to say you wouldn't regret it later?" he went on. "You've wanted to be a doctor for so many years, and frankly, I don't know if my love could satisfy you. Someday you might have been able to return to medical school—I would have wanted that for you—but my life, my business, everything I need is here in Nome. It's where I belong. But not you, Red." The affectionate endearment rolled easily from his lips, seemingly without thought. "We live in two different worlds. And my world will never satisfy you."

"What about all this business about the sign from God? You were the one who was so sure. You were the one who claimed this deep, undying love." She hurled the words at him bitterly, intent on hurting him as much as he was hurting her.

"I was wrong. I don't know how I could have done anything so stupid."

Again she had to restrain herself from crying out

that it had never been absurd, it was wonderful. The Bible verse in the mirror had meant so much to them both. But she refused to plead, and the dull ache in her heart took on a throbbing intensity.

"That's not all," he added with a cruel twist. "There's someone else now."

Nothing could have shocked her more. "Don't lie to me, Seth. Anything but that!"

"Believe it, because it's true. My situation hasn't changed. I need a wife, someone to share my life. There's"—he hesitated—"someone I was seeing before I met you. I was going to ask her to marry me as soon as I got the engagement ring back from you."

"You're lucky I brought it with me," she shouted as she tore open her purse and dumped the contents over the bedspread. Carelessly she sorted through her things. It took only a couple of seconds to locate the velvet box, turn around and viciously hurl it at Seth.

Instinctively he brought his hands up and caught the box. Their eyes met for a moment, then without another word he tucked it in his coat pocket.

A searing pain burned through her heart and she bit her lower lip.

Seth seemed to hesitate. He hovered for a moment by the door. "I didn't mean to hurt you." Slowly he lowered his gaze to meet hers.

She avoided his look. Nothing would be worse than to have him offer her sympathy. "I'm sure you didn't," she whispered on a bitter note, and her voice cracked. "Please leave," she requested urgently.

Without another word, Seth opened the door and walked away.

Numb with shock, Claudia couldn't cry, couldn't move. Holding up her head became an impossible task. A low, protesting cry came from deep within her throat, and she covered her mouth with the palm of one hand. Somehow she made it to the bed, collapsing on the mattress.

Claudia woke the next morning, and a quick lump of pain formed in her throat at the memory of her encounter with Seth. For a while she tried to force herself to return to the black cloud of mindless sleep, but to no avail.

She dressed and stared miserably out the window. The winds were blustery, but nothing compared to yesterday's gales. Seth would have returned to Kotzebue. Her world had died, but Nome lived. The city appeared calm; people were walking, laughing and talking. Claudia wondered if she would ever laugh again. What had gone wrong? Hadn't she trusted God, trusted in Seth's love? How could her world dissolve like this? The tightness in her throat grew and grew.

The small room became her prison. She waited an impatient hour, wondering what she should do, until further lingering became intolerable. Since she was here, she might as well explore the city Seth loved.

The people were friendly and offered an easy smile and a cheery good morning as she passed. There weren't any large stores, nothing to compete with Seattle. She strolled down the walkway, following the only paved road she could see. Not caring where her feet took her, she continued until she saw the sign ARCTIC BARGE COMPANY—Seth's business. A wave of fresh pain swamped her fragile composure and she turned and briskly walked in the opposite direction. Ahead, she spotted a picturesque white church with bell and steeple. Claudia sought peace inside.

The interior was dark as she slipped quietly into the back pew. Thanksgiving would be at the end of the month—a time for sharing God's goodness with family and friends. She was trapped in Nome with neither. When she'd left Seattle, her heart had nearly burst with praise for God. Now it was ready to burst with the pain of Seth's rejection.

Claudia didn't mean to cry, but there was something so peaceful and restful about the quiet church. A tear slipped from the corner of her eye and Claudia wiped it aside. She'd left Seattle so sure of Seth's love and the joy of her newfound discovery. She'd come in faith. And this was where faith had led her. To an empty church, with a heart burdened by bitter memories.

She'd painted herself into a dark corner. She'd lost her apartment. Ashley had found herself a cheaper place and a new roommate. If she did return to school, she would be forced to repeat the quarter, and there wasn't any guarantee she would be admitted back into the medical program. Every possession she owned had been carefully packed and loaded onto a barge that wouldn't arrive in Nome for months.

Claudia poured out her complications in prayer. She had come, following what she thought was God's leading, and now it seemed she had made a terrible mistake. Lifting the Bible from the pew, she sat and read, desperately seeking guidance, until she caught a movement from the corner of her eye. A stocky middle-aged man was approaching.

"Can I help you?" the man asked her softly.

Claudia looked up blankly.

He read the confusion in her eyes. "I'm Paul

Reeder, the pastor," he said to identify himself, and sat beside her in the pew.

She held out her hand and smiled weakly. "Claudia Masters."

"Your first visit to Nome?" His voice was gentle and inquiring.

"Yes, how'd you know?" she couldn't help but wonder aloud.

He grinned and his brown eyes sparkled. "Easy, I know everyone in town, and either you're a visitor or I've fallen down on my duties."

Claudia nodded and hung her head at the reminder of why and for whom she had come to Nome.

"Is there something I can do for you, child?" he asked thoughtfully.

"I don't think there's much anyone can do anymore." Her voice shook slightly, and she lowered her lashes in an effort to conceal the desperation in her eyes.

"Things are rarely as difficult as they seem. Remember, God doesn't close a door without opening a window," he said in kind understanding.

Claudia attempted a smile. "I guess I need someone to point to the window."

"Would you feel better if you confided in someone?" he urged gently.

She didn't feel up to explanations, but knew she should say something. "I quit school and moved to Alaska expecting . . . a job." The pastor was sure to know Seth, and she didn't want to involve the good man in her relationship with Seth. "I . . . I assumed wrong . . . and now . . ."

"You need a job and place to live," he concluded

for her. A light gleamed in the clear depths of the older man's eyes. "There's an apartment for rent near here. Since it belongs to the church, the payments are reasonable. As for the other problem . . ." He paused thoughtfully. "You're trained in a specific skill?"

"No, not really." The words were heavy and bare. "I have a college degree in premed and have completed one year of medical school, but other than that—"

"My dear girl!" Pastor Reeder clenched his hands in excitement. "You are the answer to our prayers. Nome desperately needs medical assistants. We've advertised for months for another doctor—"

"Oh, please understand," Claudia cried, "I'm not a doctor. I'm not even qualified to work in the medical profession. All I have is the book knowledge, but little practical experience."

Disregarding her objections, Pastor Reeder stood and anxiously moved into the wide aisle. "There's someone you must meet."

A worried frown marred Claudia's smooth brow. She licked her dry lips and followed the tall man as he briskly stepped from the church and into the street.

They stopped a block or two later. "While we're here, I'll show you the apartment." He unlocked the door to a small house and Claudia stepped inside.

"Tiny" wasn't the word; it was the most compact space Claudia had ever seen: living room, miniature kitchen and a very small bathroom.

"It's perfect," she stated positively. Perfect if she didn't have to return to Seattle and face Cooper. Perfect if she could show Seth she wasn't like a wave tossed to and fro by the sea. She had made her decision and was here to stay, with or without him. She had responded in faith; God was her guide.

"The apartment isn't on the sewer," the pastor added. "I hope that won't inconvenience you."

"Of course not." Claudia smiled. It didn't matter to her if she had a septic tank.

He nodded approvingly. "I'll arrange for water delivery, then."

Claudia didn't understand, but let the comment pass as he locked the door.

He led her down the street. "I'm taking you to meet a friend of mine, Dr. Jim Coleman. I'm sure Jim will share my enthusiasm when I tell him about your medical background."

"Shouldn't I sign something and make a deposit on the apartment first?"

Pastor Reeder's eyes twinkled. "We'll settle that later. Thanksgiving has arrived early in Nome. I can't see going through the rigmarole of deposits when God Himself has sent you to us." He handed her the key and smiled contentedly.

The doctor's waiting room was crowded with people when Claudia and Pastor Reeder entered. Every chair was taken, and small children played on the floor.

The receptionist greeted them warmly. "Good morning, Pastor. What can I do for you? Not another emergency, I hope."

"Quite the opposite. Tell Jim I'd like to see him, right away, if possible. I promise to take only a few minutes of his time."

They were ushered into a private office. The large

desk was covered with correspondence, magazines and medical journals. A pair of glasses had been carelessly tossed on top of the pile.

A young-looking doctor entered the room fifteen minutes later and skeptically eyed Claudia, dark eyes narrowed fractionally.

Eagerly Paul Reeder stood and beamed a smile toward Claudia. "Jim, I'd like to introduce you to God's Thanksgiving present to you."

Claudia stood and extended her hand. The smile on her face died as she noted the frown that flitted across the young doctor's brow.

The handshake was barely civil. "Listen, Paul, I haven't the time for your matchmaking efforts today —no matter who the young lady is. There are fifteen people in my waiting room and the hospital just phoned. Mary Fulton's in labor."

If he hadn't spoken so gruffly, Claudia could have forgiven the bad manners, but now her eyes snapped with blue sparks at the affront.

"Let me assure you, Dr. Coleman, that you are the last man I'd care to be matched with!"

A wild light flashed in Jim's eyes and it looked as if he would have stormed a reply if Pastor Reeder hadn't scrambled to his feet.

"I'll not have you insulting the woman the good Lord sent to help you. And you, Claudia"—he turned to her, waving his finger—"don't be offended. Jim made an honest mistake. He's simply overworked and rushed."

Confusion and embarrassment played rapidly over the physician's face. "The Lord sent?" he repeated. "You're a nurse?"

Sadly Claudia shook her head. "Medical student.

Ex–medical student," she corrected. "I don't know if I'll be much help; I don't have much practical skill."

"If you work with me, you'll gain that fast enough." He looked at her as if she had suddenly descended from heaven. "I've been urgently looking for someone to train to work on an emergency medical team. With your background and a few months of on-the-job training, you can take the paramedic test and easily qualify. What do you say, Claudia? Can we start again?" His boyish grin lent reassurance.

Claudia smiled reluctantly, not knowing what to say. Only minutes before, she'd claimed to be following God, responding in faith. Did He always move so quickly? "Why not?" she said with a laugh.

"Can you start tomorrow?"

"Sure," she confirmed, grateful that she would be kept so busy she wouldn't have time to remember that the reason she had come to Nome had nothing to do with paramedic training.

A message was waiting for her when she returned to the hotel. It gave a phone number and name, with information for the flights leaving Nome for Anchorage. Crumpling the paper, Claudia checked out of the hotel.

The rest of the afternoon was spent unpacking and settling in the tiny apartment. If Cooper could only see her now!

Hunger pangs interrupted her work, and Claudia realized she hadn't eaten all day. Just as she was beginning to wonder about dinner, there was a knock on the door. Her immediate thought was that Seth had somehow learned she hadn't returned to Seattle. Though it was unlikely, she realized, since Seth was in Kotzebue.

Opening the door, she found a petite blond with warm blue eyes and a friendly smile. "Welcome to Nome! I'm Barbara Reeder," she said and handed Claudia a warm plate covered with aluminum foil.

"Dad's been talking about his miracle ever since I walked in the door this afternoon, and I decided to meet this Joan of Arc myself." Her laugh was free and easy.

Claudia liked her immediately. Barbara's personality was similar to Ashley's, and the two women fell into ready conversation. Claudia let Barbara do most of the talking. She learned that the woman was close to her own age, worked as a legal secretary and was engaged to a man named Teddy. Claudia felt she needed a friend, someone bright and cheerful to lift her spirits from a tangled web of self-pity.

"Barbara, while you're here, would you mind explaining about the bathroom?" Claudia had been shocked to discover the room was missing the most important appliance.

Barbara's eyes rounded derisively. "You mean Dad didn't explain that you aren't on the sewer?"

"Yes, but—"

"Only houses on the sewers have flush toilets, plumbing and the rest. You, my newfound friend, have your very own 'honey bucket.' It's like having an indoor outhouse. When you need to use it, just open the door in the wall, pull it inside and—voilà."

Claudia looked up shocked. "Yes, but—"

"You'll need to get yourself a fuzzy cover, because the seat is freezing. When you're through, open the door, replace it outside and it'll freeze almost immediately."

"Yes, but—"

"Oh, and the water is delivered on Monday, Wednesday and Friday. Garbage is picked up once a week, but be sure and keep it inside the house because wild dogs will get into it if it's outside."

"Yes, but—"

"And I don't suppose Dad explained about ordering food supplies, either. Don't worry, I'll get you an order from the catalog and you'll have plenty of time to decide what you need. Grocery prices are sometimes as much as four times higher than Seattle, so we order the nonperishables once a year. The barge from Seattle arrives before winter."

Claudia breathed in deeply. The concepts of honey buckets, no plumbing and wild dogs were almost too much to grasp in one lump. This life-style was primitive compared to that of Seattle. But she would grow stronger from the challenges, grow or falter and break.

Concern clouded Barbara's countenance. "Have I discouraged you?"

Pride and inner strength shimmered in Claudia's eyes. "No, Nome is where I belong," she stated firmly.

Jim Coleman proved to be an excellent teacher. Her admiration for him grew with every day and every patient. At the end of her first week, Claudia was exhausted. Together they had examined and treated a steady flow of the sick and injured, eating quick lunches when they could between patients and small emergencies. At the end of the ten-to-twelve-hour day, Jim was sometimes due to report to the hospital. Claudia spent her evenings studying a huge pile of material he had given her to prepare for the paramedic exam that spring. Claudia marveled at how hard he drove himself, but Jim explained his work load wasn't by choice. Few medical staff were willing to set up practices in the frozen North.

Barbara stopped by during Claudia's second week in Nome with an invitation for Thanksgiving Day. Jim had also been invited, along with Barbara's fiancé and another couple. Claudia thanked her, accepted and might have appeared preoccupied, because Barbara left soon afterward. Claudia closed the door, leaning against the wood frame and swallowed back the bitter hurt. When she'd left Seattle, she told Ashley that she was hoping the wedding would be around Thanksgiving. Now she would spend the day with strangers.

"Good morning, Jim," she greeted the doctor cheerfully the next day. "And you, too, Mrs. Lucy."

The receptionist glanced up, grinning sheepishly to herself.

"Something funny?" Jim demanded brusquely.

"Did either of you get a chance to read Pastor Reeder's sign in front of the church this morning?" she asked.

Claudia shook her head and waited.

"What did he say this time?" Jim asked, his interest aroused.

"The sign reads: GOD WANTS SPIRITUAL FRUIT, NOT RELIGIOUS NUTS."

Jim Coleman tipped his head back and chuckled, but his face soon grew serious. "I suggest we get moving," he said. "We've got a full schedule."

Jim was right. The pace at which he drove himself and his staff left little time for chatting or visiting. With so many people in need of medical attention and only two doctors dividing the load, they had to work as efficiently as possible. At six, Claudia had barely had time to grab a sandwich. She was bandaging a badly cut hand after Jim had stitched it when he stuck his head around the corner.

"I want you to check the man in the first room. Let me know what you think. I've got a phone call waiting for me. I'll take it in my office and join you in a few minutes."

A stray curl of rich auburn hair fell haphazardly across her face, and Claudia paused long enough to tuck it around her ear and straighten the white smock.

Tapping lightly, her smile warm and automatic, she entered the room. "Good afternoon, my name's—"

Stopping short, she felt her stomach pitch wildly. Seth. His eyes were cold and hard. The thin line of his mouth tightened ominously.

"What are you doing here?"

Chapter Eight

"I work here," Claudia returned, outwardly calm, although her heartbeat was racing frantically. She had realized it would only be a matter of time before she ran into Seth, and had in fact been mildly surprised it hadn't happened before now. But nothing could have prepared her for the impact of seeing him again.

Seth's mouth tightened grimly. "Why aren't you in Seattle?" he demanded in a low growl.

"Because I'm here," she countered logically. "Why should you care if I'm in Seattle or Timbuktu? As I recall, you'd washed your hands of me," she replied defensively.

Her answer didn't please him, and Seth propelled

himself from the examination table in one angry movement. But he couldn't conceal the wince of pain as he placed his weight on the injured leg.

For the first time Claudia realized he was hurt. "Jim asked me to look at that leg—now get back on the table."

"Jim?" Seth murmured the name derisively. "You seem to have come to a first-name basis pretty quickly."

Pinching her lips tightly together, she ignored the implication. "I'm going to check you whether you like it or not," she commanded with authority few would question.

Seth's dark eyes narrowed mutinously at her demand.

Winning any kind of verbal confrontation with Seth would be almost impossible. She wouldn't have been surprised if he'd stalked from the office limping rather than follow her demand. He might well have if Jim Coleman hadn't entered the cubicle at that precise minute.

"I've been talking to the hospital," he remarked, handing Claudia the medical chart. Sheer reflex prevented the folder from falling as it slipped through her fingers. She caught it and glanced up guiltily.

Jim seemed oblivious to the thick atmosphere between the two. "Have you examined the wound?" he questioned and motioned for Seth to return to the table.

Seth hesitated for a moment before repositioning himself on the table. With another flick of his hand, Jim directed Seth to lie down. Again he paused before lowering his back onto the red vinyl cushion. He lay with his eyes closed, and Claudia thought her heart would burst. She loved this man, even when he had cast her from his life, tossing out cruel words in an attempt to make her hate him. Still, she couldn't.

Jim lifted the large bandage, allowing Claudia the first look at the angry wound. Festering with yellow pus, the cut must have been the source of constant, throbbing pain. Gently testing the skin around the infection brought a deathly pallor to Seth's face as he battled to disguise the intense pain. A faint but nonetheless distinct red line followed the cut, reaching halfway up his thigh.

"Blood poisoning," Claudia murmured gravely. She could almost feel his agony and paled slightly. Anxiously she glanced at Jim.

"Blood poisoning or not, just give me the medicine and let me out of here. I've got a business to run. I can't be held up here all day while you two ohh and ahh over a minor cut." The sharp words burst impatiently from Seth as he struggled to sit upright.

"You seem to think you can work with that wound," Jim shot back angrily. "Go ahead if you fancy strapping a wooden peg to your hip the rest of your life. You need to be in the hospital."

"So you keep saying," Seth retorted.

Stiff with concern, Claudia stepped forward when Seth let out a low moan and lay back down.

"Do whatever you have to," he said in a resigned tone.

"I'd like to talk to you in my office a minute, Claudia. Go ahead and wait for me there."

The request surprised her, but she did as Jim asked. He joined her a moment later, a frown of concern twisted his brow.

"I've already spoken to the hospital," he announced and slumped defeatedly into his chair. "There aren't any beds available." He ran a hand over his face and looked up at her with unseeing eyes. "It's times like these that make me wonder why I chose to work in Nome. Inadequate facilities, no private nurses, overworked staff . . . I don't know how much more of these hours my health will take."

Claudia hadn't known Jim long, but she had never seen him more frustrated or angry.

"I've contacted the airport to have him flown out by a charter plane, but there's a storm coming and flying for the next twelve hours would be suicidal," Jim continued. "His leg can't wait that long. Something's got to be done before that infection spreads any farther." He straightened and released a bitter sigh. "I don't have any choice but to send you home with him, Claudia. He's going to need constant care, or he could lose that leg. I can't do it myself, and there's no one else I would trust."

Claudia leaned against the door, needing its support as the weight of responsibility pressed heavily upon her shoulders. She couldn't refuse.

Patiently Jim outlined the treatment for the infection. His eyes studied Claudia for a sign of confusion or misunderstanding. He gave her the supplies and reminded her of the seriousness of the infection.

An hour later, with Seth strongly protesting, Claudia managed to get him into his home and into his bed. Propping his leg up with a pillow, she removed the bandage to view the open wound a second time. She cringed at the sight of the rotting flesh and fought back revulsion.

Her eyes clouded with worry as she worked gently and efficiently to make him as comfortable as possible. Purposefully she avoided his gaze in an attempt to mask her concern.

He appeared somewhat more comfortable as he rested his head against the pillow. The only sign of pain he allowed to show on the ruggedly carved features was the tightly clenched mouth. Beads of perspiration wetted his brow. Claudia didn't need to see his agony to know he was in intense pain.

"Why are you here?" He repeated his earlier question, his eyes closed.

"I'm taking care of your leg," she replied gently. "Don't talk now, try and sleep if you can." Deftly she opened the bag of supplies and laid them out on the dresser table.

Standing above him, she rested her cool hand against his heated brow.

At the tender touch of her fingers, he raised his hand and gripped her wrist. "Don't play games with me, Red." He opened his eyes to hold her gaze. "Why are you in Nome?" The words were weak; there wasn't any fight left in him. Protesting Jim's arrangements had depleted him of strength. Now every effort was used to disguise his pain. "Have you come back to torment me?"

"I never left," she answered and touched a finger to his lips to prevent his questions. "Not now," she whispered. "We'll talk later and I'll explain then."

He nodded almost imperceptibly and rolled his head to the side.

Examining the cut brought a liquid sheen to her eyes. "How could you have let this go so long?" she protested. Jim had explained to her earlier that Seth had fallen against a cargo crate while in Kotzebue. Claudia recalled that he had a slight limp the day he had picked her up from the airport. He had let the injury go untreated all that time. Was he crazy?

He didn't respond to her question, but exhaled a sharp breath as she gently began swabbing the wound. To cause him the least amount of pain, she probed the wound patiently. She bit into her lip when he winced again, but it was important to clean the cut and check the possibility of foreign matter imbedded in the flesh. Jim had given Seth antibiotics and pain-killers before leaving the office, but their effect had been minor.

When she'd finished, she heated hot water in the kitchen, steeping strips of cloth in the clean water. Allowing them to cool slightly, she placed the cloths over his thigh. His body jerked taut and his mouth tightened with the renewed effort to conceal his torment. The process was repeated until the wound was thoroughly cleansed. Claudia returned to the kitchen.

"I'm going to lose this leg," Seth mumbled as she walked into the bedroom.

"Not if I can help it," she said with a determination that produced a weak smile from him.

"I'm glad you're here," he said, his voice fading.

Claudia gently squeezed his hand. "I'm glad I'm here, too." Even if she did return to Seattle, there would always be the satisfaction of having been able to help Seth.

He rested fitfully. Some time later, she again heated water, adding the medicine Jim had given her to the steaming water. A pungent odor filled the room. As quietly as possible, so not to disturb him, she again steeped the strips. Cautiously she draped them around the swollen leg, securing them with a large plastic bag to keep them moist and warm as long as possible. When the second stage of Jim's instructions had been completed, she slumped wearily into a chair at Seth's bedside.

Two hours later she repeated the process, and again after another two-hour interval. Claudia didn't know what time it was when Jim came. But there didn't seem to be any noticeable improvement in Seth's condition.

"How's the fever?" Jim asked as he checked the sleeping man's pulse.

"High," Claudia replied, unable to conceal her worry.

"Give him time," Jim cautioned. He gave Seth another injection and glanced at his watch. "I'm due at the hospital. I'll see what I can do to find someone to replace you."

"No!" she said abruptly, too abruptly. "I'll stay."

Jim eyed her curiously, his gaze searching. "You've been at this several hours now. The next few could be crucial, and I don't want you working yourself sick."

"I'm going to see him through this," she said with marked determination. Avoiding the question in his eyes, she made busy work around the room. She would answer him later if she must, but now all that mattered was Seth and getting him well.

Jim left a few minutes later, and Claudia paused to fix herself something to eat. She would need her strength, but although she tried to force herself to eat, her fears mounted, dispelling her appetite.

The ache in the small of her back throbbed as she continued to labor through the night. Again and again she applied the hot cloths to draw out the poison.

Claudia bit at her lip anxiously when she took his temperature and discovered the fever continued to rage, despite her efforts. Her fingers gently tested the flesh surrounding the infection, and she frowned heavily.

Waves of panic mounted again a few minutes later when Seth stirred restlessly in his sleep. He rolled his head slowly from side to side as the pain disturbed his sleep.

"Jesus, please help us," Claudia prayed as she grew more dismayed. Nothing she did seemed to be able to control Seth's fever.

Repeatedly she'd heard the importance of remaining calm and clear-headed when treating a patient. But her heart was filled with dread as the hours passed, each one interminable, and still his fever raged. If she couldn't lower Seth's fever, he might lose his leg.

His Bible lay on the nightstand and Claudia picked it up, holding it in both hands. She brought the leather-bound book to her breast and lifted her eyes to heaven, murmuring a fervent prayer.

Another hour passed and he began to moan and mumbled incoherently as he slipped into a feverish delirium. He tossed his head and Claudia was forced to hold him down as he struggled, flinging out his arms.

He quieted and Claudia tenderly stroked his brow while whispering soothing words of comfort in an attempt to quiet him.

Unexpectedly, with an amazing strength, Seth jerked upright and cried out in anguish, "John . . . watch out . . . no . . . no . . ."

Gently but firmly she laid him back against the pillow, murmuring softly in an effort to calm him. Absently she wondered who John was. She couldn't remember Seth ever mentioning anyone by that name.

Repeatedly he mumbled something about John. Once he even laughed, the laugh she loved so much. But only seconds later he again cried out in anguish.

Tears that had been lingering so close to the surface quickly welled. Loving someone, as she loved Seth, made that person's torment one's own. Never had she loved this completely, this strongly.

"Hush, my darling," she murmured softly.

She was afraid to leave him, even for a moment, so she pulled the chair as close as she could to his bedside and sank wearily into it. Exhaustion claimed her mind to everything but prayer.

Toward daylight, Seth seemed to be resting more comfortably and Claudia slipped into a light sleep.

Someone spoke her name and she shifted from her uncomfortable position to find Seth, eyes open, regarding her steadily.

"Good morning," he whispered weakly. His forehead and face were beaded with sweat, his shirt damp with perspiration. The fever, at last, had broken.

A lump of happiness formed in Claudia's throat and she offered an immediate prayer of thanksgiving.

"Good morning," she returned the greeting, her voice light as relief washed over her. She beamed with joy as she tested his forehead. It felt moist and cool, and she stood to wipe the sweat from his face with a fresh washcloth.

His hand stopped her action and closed over her fingers, as if touching her would prove she was real. "I'm not dreaming, it is you."

She laughed softly. "The one and only." Suddenly

conscious of her disheveled appearance, Claudia ran her fingers through her tangled hair and straightened her blouse.

His warm gaze watched her movements and Claudia felt unexpectedly shy.

"You told me you never left Nome." The inflection in his voice made the statement a question.

"I didn't come here to turn around and go back home," she said and smiled, allowing all the pent-up love to burn in her eyes.

His eyes questioned her as she examined his leg. The improvement was remarkable. She smiled, remembering her frantic prayers during the night. Only the Great Physician could have worked this quickly.

She helped Seth sit up and removed his damp shirt. They worked together silently as she wiped him down and slipped a fresh shirt over his head. Taking the bowl, and tucking his shirt under her arm, she smiled at him and walked toward the door.

"Red, don't go," he called urgently.

"I'll be right back," she assured him. "I'm just going to take these into the kitchen and fix you something to eat."

"Not now." He extended his hand to her, his look intense. "We need to talk."

Claudia walked back to the dresser to deposit the bowl before moving to the bed. Their eyes locked as they studied one another. A radiant glow of love seemed to reach out to her. She took his hand in her own and, raising it to her face, rested it against her cheek and closed her eyes. She didn't resist as the pressure of his arm pulled her downward. She knelt on the carpet beside the bed and was wrapped in his embrace.

Seth's breathing was heavy and labored as he buried his face in the gentle slope of her neck. This was what she'd needed, what she'd yearned for from the minute she stepped off the plane—Seth and the assurance of his love.

"I've been a fool," he muttered thickly.

"We both have. But I'm here now, and it's going to take a lot more than some angry words to pry me out of your arms." She pulled slightly away so she'd be able to look at him as she spoke. "If there's anyone to blame, then it's me," she murmured and brushed the hair from the sides of his face. He captured her hand and pressed a kiss against her palm. "I'd never once told you I loved you."

His hand tightened around hers punishingly. "You love me?"

"Very much." She confirmed her words with a nod of her head. "You told me so many times that you needed me, but I discovered it was I who needed you."

"Why didn't you tell me when you arrived that you intended to stay?" He met her eyes, and she watched as his eyes filled with regret. "I thought this was another one of your pen-pal ideas."

"I'm a little slow sometimes," she said. She sat in the chair but continued to hold his hand in hers. "I couldn't seem to understand why God would give you a sign and me nothing. I was miserable—the indecision was disrupting my whole life. Then one day I decided to read the passage you'd talked about in Genesis. I read about Abraham's servant and learned that Rebekah had come by her choice. It was as if God was offering me the same type of decision and asking that I respond in faith. It didn't take me long to recognize how much I loved you. I can't understand why I fought it so long. Once I admitted it to myself, quitting school and leaving Seattle became secondary."

"You quit school?"

"Without even hesitating." She laughed with sudden amusement. "I'd make a rotten doctor. Haven't you noticed that I become emotionally involved with my patients?"

"What about your uncle?" Seth questioned wryly.

"He's accepted my decision. He's not happy about it, but I think he understands more than he lets on."

"We'll make him godfather to our first son," Seth said and slipped a large hand around her nape, pulling her trembling, soft mouth across the narrow distance to meet his. The kiss was so gentle that tears misted her eyes. Seth's hands framed each side of her face as his mouth slanted across hers, the contact deepening until he seemed capable of drawing out her soul.

Jim Coleman stopped by later, but only long enough to quickly check Seth's leg and give him another injection of antibiotic. He spoke frankly with Seth and warned him it would take weeks to regain the full use of the leg.

He hesitated once, apparently noticing the silent communication and love that flashed between Seth and Claudia. His eyes narrowed and the corner of his mouth twitched. For a fleeting moment Claudia thought the look was filled with contempt. She dismissed the idea as part of a long night and an overactive imagination. Jim left shortly afterward and promised to return that evening.

Claudia heated a lunch for both Seth and herself

and waited until he had eaten. He fell asleep while she washed the dishes. When she checked on him later, Claudia's heart swelled with the wonder and joy of their love. How many other, married couples had such a profound confirmation of their lives together as Seth and she did? Seth had spoken of a son, and Claudia realized how much she wanted this man's child.

Smiling, she rested her hands lightly on the flat surface of her stomach and again entertained the thought of children. They would have tall lean sons with thick dark hair, and perhaps a daughter. A glorious happiness stole through her.

Content that Seth would sleep, she opened the other bedroom door, crawled into the bed and drifted into a deep sleep. Her dreams were happy, confident of the many years she would share with Seth.

When she awoke later, she rolled over and glanced at the clock. Seven. She had slept almost five hours. Sitting up, she stretched, lifting her arms high above her head, and rotated her neck to ease the tired muscles.

The house was quiet as she threw back the covers and walked back to Seth's room. He was awake, his face turned toward the wall. Something prevented her from speaking and drawing attention to herself. He looked troubled, worried. His face was tight. Was he in pain? Was there something to cause him concern about his business?

As if feeling her regard, Seth turned his head and their eyes met. The look was gone immediately, replaced by a loving glance that sent waves of happiness through her.

"Hello. Have you been awake long?" she asked softly.

"About an hour. What about you?"

"Just a few minutes." She moved inside the room. "Is something troubling you, Seth? You had a strange look just now, I don't exactly know how to describe it . . . a sadness?"

His hand reached for hers. "It's nothing, my love."

Her fingers tested his brow, which was cool, and she smiled contentedly. "I don't know about you, but I'm starved. I think I'll see what I can dig up in the kitchen."

Seth nodded absently.

As Claudia left the room, she couldn't help glancing over her shoulder. Her instincts told her that something wasn't right. But what?

A freshly baked pie was on the kitchen table, and Claudia glanced at it curiously. When did that appear? She shrugged her shoulders and opened the refrigerator. Maybe Seth had some eggs and she could make an omelette. There weren't any eggs, but a gelatin salad sat prominently on the top shelf. Again Claudia felt a prickling of something out of place. When she turned around, she noted that the oven light was on, and a quick look through the glass door showed a casserole dish warming. Someone had been to the house when she'd been asleep and brought Seth a meal. How thoughtful.

"You didn't tell me you had company," she said as she carried a tray into the bedroom for Seth.

He was sitting on the edge of the mattress and she

could see him tightly grit his teeth as he attempted to stand.

"Seth, don't," she cried and quickly set the tray down to hurry to his side. "You shouldn't be out of bed."

He sank back onto the side of the mattress and closed his eyes to mask an influx of pain. "You know, I think you're right about that."

"Here, let me help you." With an arm around his shoulders, she gently lifted the injured leg and propped it against a thick pillow. When she'd finished, she turned to Seth and smiled. She couldn't hide the soft glow that warmed her eyes as she looked upon this man she loved.

Sitting up, his back supported by pillows, Seth held his arms out to her and drew her into his embrace. His mouth sought hers, and the kisses spoke more of passion than gentleness. But Claudia didn't care. She returned his kisses, linking her hands around his neck, her fingers exploring the black hair at the base of his head. His hands moved intimately over her back as if he couldn't have enough of her.

"I think your recovery will impress Dr. Coleman, especially if he could see us now," she teased and tried to laugh. But the husky tone betrayed the extent of her arousal. When Seth kissed her again, hard and long, she offered no resistance.

Crushed in his embrace, held immobile by the steel band that circled her waist, she submitted happily to the mastery of his kisses.

Claudia smiled happily into his gleaming eyes. "There are only a few more days before Thanksgiving," she murmured and kissed his brow. "I have so much to thank God for this year—more happiness than one woman was ever meant to have. I had hoped when I first came that we might be married Thanksgiving week; it seemed fitting somehow." There were no more doubts, she was utterly his.

Although Seth continued to hold her, she felt again the stirring sense of something amiss. When she leaned her head back to glance at him, she noted that his look was distant, preoccupied.

"Seth, is something wrong?" she asked a second time.

A smile of reassurance touched his lips, but Claudia noted that it didn't reach his eyes. "Everything's fine."

"Are you hungry?"

He nodded eagerly and straightened so that she could bring him the tray. "I'm always hungry."

But he hardly touched his meal.

She brought him a cup of coffee from the kitchen after taking away the dinner tray. She sat beside him in the chair, her hands cupping the hot mug.

"If you don't object, I'd like Pastor Reeder to marry us," she said and took a sip of the hot liquid.

"You know Paul Reeder?" His eyes shot over her curiously.

Claudia nodded. "I'm very grateful for his friendship. He's the one who introduced me to Jim Coleman. He also rented me the apartment the church owns—honey bucket and all," she said with a tender smile. "I'm going to like Nome. There are some wonderful people here. I found the dinner in the kitchen; it wouldn't surprise me if Pastor Reeder had something to do with that."

"He did," Seth confirmed. "Paul's the one who

talked to me about Christ and salvation. I greatly respect the man."

"I suspected as much." Claudia recalled Seth's telling her about the pastor who had led him to Christ. From the first day, Claudia had suspected it was Pastor Reeder. "I didn't get to church last Sunday to hear him preach, but I bet he packs a powerful sermon."

"He does," Seth said and looked away.

Claudia's gaze followed his and she noticed that Jim Coleman had let himself into the house. The two men eyed each other and an icy stillness seemed to fill the room. Claudia looked from one man to the other and lightly shook her head, sure she was imagining things.

"I think you'll be impressed with how well Seth is doing," she said and moved aside so Jim could examine the cut himself.

Neither man spoke and the tension in the room was so thick that Claudia found herself stiffening. Something was wrong between these two, something was very wrong.

Claudia walked Jim to the front door. Again he praised her efforts. "He might have lost that leg if it hadn't been for you."

"I was glad to help," she said, studying him a second time. "But I feel God had more to do with the improvement than I did."

"That could be." He shrugged and expelled a long, tired sigh. "He should be okay by himself tonight if you want to go home and get a good night's sleep."

"I might," she responded noncommittally.

Jim nodded and turned to leave. Claudia stopped

him with a hand on his arm. "Jim, something's going on between you and Seth."

"Did he tell you that?"

"No."

"Then ask him," he said, casting a wary glance in Seth's direction.

"I will," she replied, determined to do just that.

Seth's eyes were closed when she returned to his room, but she wasn't fooled. "Don't you like Jim Coleman?" she asked right out.

"He's a fine Christian man. There aren't many doctors as dedicated as he is."

"But you don't like him, do you?"

Seth closed his eyes again and let out a sharp breath. "I don't think it's a question of my friendship. Jim doesn't like me and at the moment I can't blame him," he responded cryptically.

Claudia didn't know what to say. It was obvious Seth didn't want to talk about it, and she didn't feel she should pry. It hurt a little that he wouldn't confide in her. There wasn't anything she would ever keep from him. But she couldn't and wouldn't force it, not if he wasn't ready.

An hour later she checked on Seth, who appeared to be asleep. Leaning down, she kissed his brow. She was undecided about spending another night. A hot shower and a fresh change of clothes sounded tempting.

"Seth," she whispered, and he stirred. "I'm going home for the night. I'll see you early tomorrow morning."

"No." He sat up and winced, seeming to have forgotten his leg. "Don't go, Red. Stay tonight. You can leave in the morning if you want." He reached for her, holding her so tight she ached.

"Okay, my love," she whispered tenderly. "Just call if you need me."

"I'll need you all my life. Don't ever forget that, Red."

He sounded so adamant that she frowned, drawing her delicate brows together. "I won't forget."

Claudia woke before Seth the next morning. She was in the kitchen putting on a pot of coffee when she heard a car pull up outside the kitchen door.

Barbara Reeder slammed the car door closed and waved. Claudia returned the wave and opened the door for her friend.

"You're out bright and early this morning," she said cheerfully. "I just put on coffee."

"Morning." Barbara returned the smile. "How's the patient?"

"Great. It's amazing how much better he is from just two days ago."

"I was sorry to miss you yesterday." Barbara pulled out a chair and set her purse on the table while she unbuttoned her parka.

"Miss me?" Claudia quizzed.

"Yes, I brought by dinner, and you were in the bedroom sound asleep. From what I understand, you were up all night. You must have been exhausted. I didn't want to wake you."

"Funny Seth didn't say anything." Claudia spoke her thoughts out loud.

Barbara's look showed mild surprise. "You don't know, do you?"

"Know what?"

"That man, honestly!" A bright bubble of happiness gleamed from her eyes. "You'd think it was top secret or something." She held out her left hand for Claudia to admire the sparkling diamond. "Teddy and I are going to be married next month."

Chapter Nine

"Teddy?" Claudia repeated. Her stomach felt as if someone had kicked her. Somehow she managed to conceal her shock.

"It's confusing, I know," Barbara responded with a happy laugh. "But Seth has always reminded me of a teddy bear. He's so big and cuddly, it seemed only natural to call him Teddy."

Claudia's hand shook as she poured coffee into two mugs. Barbara continued to chat excitedly about her wedding plans, stating they'd hoped to have the wedding before Christmas.

Strangely, Claudia felt no emotion. She sipped her coffee, adding little to the conversation. Barbara didn't seem to notice.

"Teddy changed after John's death," Barbara added and blew into the side of her mug.

"John," Claudia repeated the name. Seth had called out the name several times while his fever raged.

"John was his younger brother, and partner in Arctic Barge. There was some kind of accident on a barge—I'm not sure I ever got the story straight. Seth was with John when it happened. Something fell on top of him and ruptured his heart. He died in Seth's arms."

Claudia stared into the coffee. From that first day she'd walked into the Wilderness Motel, she'd known there was a terrible sadness in Seth's life. She'd felt it even then. But he had never shared his grief with her. As much as he professed to love her and want her for his wife, he hadn't shared the deepest part of himself. Knowing this hurt as much as his engagement to Barbara.

"Could I ask a favor of you?" Claudia said and stood, placing her mug in the kitchen sink. "Would you mind dropping me off at my apartment? I don't want to take Seth's car, since I don't know when I'll be back. It should only take a minute."

"Of course. Then I'll come back and surprise Seth with breakfast."

He'd be amazed all right, Claudia couldn't help musing.

She managed to maintain a fragile poise until Barbara dropped her off. Waving her thanks, she entered her tiny home. She looked around the room that had so quickly become her own and bit the inside of her cheek. With purposeful strides she opened the lone closet and pulled out her suitcases. She folded each garment with unhurried care and placed it neatly inside the leather luggage.

Someone knocked at the door, but Claudia obstinately ignored the repeated raps.

"Open up, Claudia, I know you're in there. I saw Barbara drop you off." It was Jim Coleman.

"Go away," she cried, and her voice cracked. A tear squeezed past her determination not to cry, and she angrily wiped it away with the back of her hand.

Ignoring her lack of welcome, Jim pushed open the door and stepped inside the room.

"I like the way people respect my privacy around here," she bit out sarcastically. "I don't feel up to company at the moment, Jim. Another time, maybe." She turned around and continued packing.

"I want you to listen to me for a minute." Clearly he was angry.

"No, I won't listen. Not to anyone. Go away, just go away." She pulled the drawer from the dresser, flipped it over and emptied the contents into the last suitcase.

"Will you stop acting like a lunatic and listen? You can't leave now."

She whirled around and placed both hands challengingly on her hips. "Can't leave? You just watch me. I don't care where the next plane's going, I'll be on it," she shot out, then choked on a sob.

Jim took her in his arms. Claudia struggled at first, but he deflected her hands and held her gently. "Let it out," he whispered soothingly.

Again she tried to jerk away, but, undeterred, Jim held her fast, murmuring comforting words.

"You knew all along, didn't you?" Hurt, questioning eyes lifted to search his face.

Jim arched one brow and shrugged his shoulders. "Not until yesterday. No one could help looking at the two of you without knowing you're in love. I was on my way to his house this morning when I saw Barbara with you. Something about the way you were tilting your head told me you must have found out the truth. Did you say anything to Barbara?"

Claudia shook her head. "No. I couldn't. Why does it have to be Barbara?" she asked unreasonably. "Why couldn't it be some anonymous soul I could hate? But she's bright and cheerful, fun to be around. And she's so in love with him. You should have heard her talk about the wedding."

"I have," Jim stated and rammed his hands into his pockets. He walked to the other side of the couch that served as Claudia's bed.

"I'm not going to burst that bubble of happiness. I don't think Seth knows what he wants. He's confused and unsure. The only thing I can do is leave."

Jim turned and regarded her steadily. "You can't go now. You don't seem to understand what having you in Nome means to me, to all of us. When Pastor Reeder said you were God's Thanksgiving gift to us, he wasn't teasing. I've been praying for someone like you for months." He heaved a sigh, his eyes pleading with hers. "For the first time in weeks I've been able to do some of the paper work that's cluttering my desk. And I was planning to take a day off next week, the first one in three months."

"But you don't know what you're asking." Haunted eyes returned his pleading look.

"I do. Listen, if it will make things easier, I could marry you."

The proposal was issued sincerely, and his gaze didn't waver as he waited for her reaction.

Claudia smiled her appreciation. "Now you're being ridiculous."

Jim's taut features relaxed, and Claudia laughed outright at how relieved he looked.

"Will you stay a bit longer, at least until someone answers our advertisements in the medical journal? Two, three months at the most."

Gesturing weakly with one hand, Claudia nodded. She was in an impossible position. She couldn't stay, and she couldn't leave. And still there was Seth to face.

Jim sighed gratefully and smoothed the hair at the side of his head. "Thank you. I promise you won't regret it." He glanced at his watch. "I'm going to talk to Seth. Something's got to be done."

Claudia walked him to the door. "Why haven't you married?" His proposal prompted the question.

"Too busy in medical school," he explained. "And since I've been here, there hasn't been the time to date the one I wanted." He pulled his car keys from his pocket.

There was something strange about the way he spoke, or maybe it was the look in his eyes. Claudia stopped him by placing a hand on his arm. "You're in love with Barbara, aren't you?" If she hadn't been caught in her own problems, she would have realized it long before. Whenever Jim talked about Barbara there had been a softness in his tone.

He began to deny his feelings, but seemed to notice the knowing look in Claudia's blue eyes. "A lot of good it's done me." His shoulders slouched forward in defeat. "I'm nothing more than a family friend. Barbara's been in love with Seth for so long, she doesn't even know I'm around. And with the hours I'm forced to work, there hasn't been time to let her know how I feel."

"Does Seth love her?" Pride demanded that she hold her chin high.

"I don't know. But he must have some genuine affection for her or he wouldn't have proposed."

Both became introspective, unable to find the words to comfort each other. Jim walked out the door a minute later and Claudia stood at the window watching him go.

Clothes were scattered across the carpeted floor and she bent down to clean away the mess she'd made. As she replaced each item in the closet or the drawers, Claudia tried to pray. God had brought her to Nome. She had come believing she would marry Seth. Did God have other plans for her now that she was here? How could she bear to live in the same city when she loved Seth so completely? How could she bear seeing him married to another?

No sooner had the last suitcase been tucked away when there was another knock at the door.

Barbara's cheerful smile greeted her as she stuck her head in the front door. "Are you busy?"

Claudia had her back turned and bit into her lip. Barbara was the last person she wanted to see. It would almost be preferable to face Seth. Inwardly she groaned as she turned, forcing a smile onto her frozen lips.

"Sure, come in."

Barbara let herself in and held out a large gift-wrapped box to Claudia. "I know you're probably exhausted and this is a bad time, but I wanted to give this to you now, before I went back to Teddy's."

Numbly Claudia took the gift, unable to look higher than the bright pink bow that decorated the box. Words seemed to knot in her throat.

"I'll only stay a minute," Barbara confirmed. "Jim Coleman came by. It looked like he wanted to see Teddy alone for a few minutes, and I thought this was the perfect time to run this over."

"What is it?" The words sounded strange even to herself.

"Just a little something to show my appreciation for all you've done for Teddy. All along, Dad's said that God sent you to us. You've only been here a short time and already you've affected all our lives. Teddy could have lost his leg if it hadn't been for you. And Dad said your being here will save Jim from work exhaustion. All that aside, I see you as a very special sister the Lord sent to me. I can't remember a time I've felt closer to anyone more quickly." She ended with a shaky laugh. "Look at me," she mumbled, wiping a tear from the corner of her eye. "I'm going to start crying in a minute, and that's all we both need. Now go ahead and open the gift."

Claudia sat and rested the large box on her knees. Carefully she tore away the ribbon and paper. The ever tightening lump in her throat constricted painfully. Lifting the lid, she discovered a beautiful hand-crocheted afghan in bold autumn colors of gold, orange, yellow and brown. She couldn't restrain the gasp of pleasure. "Oh, Barbara!" She lifted it from the box and marveled at the weeks of work that had gone into its making. "I can't accept this—it's too much." She blinked rapidly in an effort to forestall the tears.

"It's hardly enough," Barbara contradicted. "God sent you to Nome as a helper to Jim, a friend to me and a nurse for my Teddy."

A low moan of protest and guilt escaped Claudia's parched throat. She couldn't refuse the gift, just as she couldn't explain why she'd come to Nome.

"How . . . how long have you been engaged?" she asked in a choked whisper.

"Only a short time. In fact, Teddy didn't give me the ring until a few days ago."

Claudia's gaze lowered to rest on the sparkling rainbow-hued diamond. She felt a sense of release that it wasn't the same ring he'd offered her.

"His proposal had to be about the most unromantic you can imagine," she said with a girlish smile. "I didn't need a fortune-teller to realize he's in love with someone else."

Claudia's breathing became shallow. "Why would you marry someone when he . . ." She couldn't finish the sentence and, unable to meet Barbara's gaze, she fingered the afghan on her lap.

"It sounds strange, doesn't it?" Barbara answered with a question. "But I love him, I have for years. We've talked about this other girl. She's someone he met on a business trip. She wasn't willing to leave everything behind for Teddy and Nome. Whoever she is, she's a fool. The affection Teddy has for me will grow, and together we'll build a good marriage. He wants children right away."

With a determined effort Claudia was able to smile.

"You'll make him a wonderful wife. And you're right, the other girl was a terrible fool." Her mouth twitched with the effort of maintaining a smile.

Again Barbara misread the look of strain in Claudia's pale face as fatigue. Standing, she slipped her arms into the thick coat. "I imagine Jim's done by now. I'd better go, but we'll get together soon. And don't forget Thanksgiving dinner. You're our guest of honor."

Claudia felt sick to her stomach and stood unsteadily. The guest of honor? This was too much.

Together they walked the short space to the door.

"Thank you again for the beautiful gift," Claudia murmured in a wavering breath.

"No, Claudia, I need to thank you. And for so much—you saved the leg of the man I love."

"You should thank God for that, not me."

"I do!"

Barbara was halfway out the door when Claudia blurted out, "What do you think of Jim Coleman?" She hadn't meant to be so abrupt and quickly averted her face.

To her surprise, Barbara stepped inside the door and laughed softly. "I told Dad a romance would soon be brewing between the two of you. It's inevitable, I suppose, working together every day. The attraction between you must be a natural thing. I think Jim's a great guy, not that I fancy his sort. He's too arrogant for my tastes. But you two are exactly right for one another. Jim needs someone like you to mellow his attitudes." A smile twinkled from the blue eyes. "We'll talk more about Jim later. I've got to get back, Teddy will be wondering what's going on. He hadn't wakened when Jim arrived, and I haven't had a chance to talk to him yet."

That afternoon Jim phoned and asked if Claudia could meet him at the office. An outbreak of flu had apparently hit Nome and several families had been affected. He needed her help immediately.

Several hours later, Claudia was exhausted. She came home and cooked a meal, then didn't eat. She washed the already clean dishes and listened to a radio broadcast until she realized it wasn't in English.

The hot water in her bathtub was steaming when there was yet another knock at her door. The temptation to let it pass and pretend she hadn't heard was strong. She didn't feel up to another chat with either Barbara or Jim. Again the knock came, this time more insistent.

Impatiently she stalked across the floor and jerked open the door. Her irritation died the minute she saw that it was Seth. He was leaning heavily on a cane, his leg causing him obvious pain.

"What are you doing here?" she demanded. "Oh, you fool!" she cried in alarm. "You shouldn't be walking on that leg."

Lines of strain were etched beside his mouth. "Then invite me inside so I can sit down." He spoke tightly and Claudia moved aside, a hand at his elbow as she helped him to the couch.

Relief was evident when he lowered himself onto it. "We have to talk, Red," he whispered coaxingly, his eyes seeking hers.

Fearing the powerful pull of his gaze, she turned away. The control he had over her senses was frightening.

"No, I think I understand everything."

"You couldn't possibly understand," Seth countered.

"Talk all you like, but it isn't going to change things." She moved to the tiny kitchen and poured water into the kettle to heat. He stood and followed her, unable to hide the grimace of pain as he moved.

"Where are you going?" he demanded.

"Sit down, Superman," she snapped. The sign of his pain upset her more than she cared to reveal. "I'm making us something to drink; it looks like we can both use it." She moved across the room and gestured toward the bathroom door. "Now I'm going to get a pair of slippers. My feet are cold." She'd taken off her shoes and the floor was chilly against her bare feet. "Any objections?"

"Plenty, but I doubt that they'll do any good."

Claudia was glad for the respite as she slipped her feet into the shoes. She felt defenseless and naked. Seth knew her too well. The room was quiet and still and she paused to pray. Her mind was crowded with a thousand questions.

"Are you coming out of there, or do I have to knock that door down?" he demanded in a harsh tone.

"I'm coming." A few seconds later she left the bathroom and entered the kitchen to pour their coffee.

His cane hit the floor. "I can't take this. Yell, scream, rant, rave, call me names, but for goodness' sake, don't treat me like this. As if you didn't care, as if you weren't dying on the inside, when I know you must be."

She licked her dry lips and handed him the steaming cup. "I don't need to yell, or scream. I admit I might have done this morning when I talked to Barbara, but not now. I have a fairly good understanding of the situation. I don't blame you, there was no way for you to know I was coming to Nome to stay." Purposely she sat across the room from him, her composure stilted as her fingers hugged the hot mug.

"Look at me, Red," he ordered softly.

She raised unsure eyes to meet his, and all time came to a halt. The unquestionable love that glowed in his dark eyes was her undoing. Claudia vaulted to her feet and turned away from him before the anguish of her own eyes became readable.

"No," she murmured brokenly.

His large hand reached for her, but she easily sidestepped his arm.

"Don't touch me, Seth."

"I love you, Claudia Masters." His words were coaxing and low.

"Don't say that!" she burst out in a half-sob.

"Don't look! Don't touch! Don't love!" His voice was sharp and marked with determination. "You're mine. I'm not going to let you go."

"I'm not yours," she cut in swiftly. "You don't own me. What about Barbara? I won't see you hurt her like this. She loves you, she'll make you a good wife. You were right about me. I don't belong here. I should be in Seattle with my family, back in medical school. I should never have come."

"That's not true and you know it," he said harshly.

"Answer me something, Seth." She paused and her lips trembled. For a moment she found it difficult to continue. "Why didn't you tell me about your brother?"

If possible, Seth paled all the more. "How do you know about John? Barbara?"

Claudia shook her head. "You called out to him in your fever the first night I tended your leg. Then Barbara said something later and I asked her."

He covered his face with his hands. "I don't like to talk about it, Red. It's something I want to forget. That feeling of utter helplessness, watching the life flow out of John. I would have told you in time. To be frank, it hasn't been a year and I still have trouble talking about it." He straightened and wiped a hand across his face. "In some ways John's death has been one of the most influential events of my life. Later, I could find no reason why I should live and my brother die. It didn't make sense. Other than the business, my life lacked purpose. I sought only personal gain and satisfaction. That was when I talked to Pastor Reeder to seek some answers and later accepted Jesus Christ. It was one of the things that made me decide it was time to get married and have a family."

Unable to speak, Claudia nodded. She had been with him that night as he relived the torment of his brother's death. She had witnessed just a little of the effect it had had upon his life.

"I'll be leaving Nome in a couple of months. I want—"

"No." Seth objected strenuously.

"I'm going back to Seattle," she continued. "And someday, with God's help, I'll be one of Washington's finest pediatricians."

"Red, I admit I've made a terrible mess of this

thing. When I told you God and I were working on the patience part of me, I wasn't kidding." His voice was low and tense. "But I can't let you go, not when I love you. Not when . . ."

"Not when Barbara's wearing your ring," she finished for him.

"Barbara . . ." he began heatedly, then stopped, defeated. "I have to talk to her. She's a wonderful woman, and I don't want to hurt her."

Claudia laughed softly. "We're both fools, aren't we? I think that at the end of three months we'd be at each other's throats." She marveled at how calm she sounded.

"You're going to marry me." Hard resolve flashed from his eyes.

"No, Seth, I'm not. There's nothing anyone can say that will prevent me from leaving."

Seth met her look and for the first time Claudia noticed the red stain on his pant leg. Her composure flew. "Your wound has opened. It was crazy for you to have come here," she cried in a shrill voice. "I've got to get you home and back into bed."

"You enjoy giving orders, don't you?" He bit out savagely. "Marry Barbara. Go home. Stay in bed." He sounded suddenly weary, as if the effort had become too much. "I'll leave, but you can be sure that we're not through discussing the subject."

"As far as I'm concerned, we are." She ripped her coat off the hanger and got her purse.

"What are you doing now?"

"Taking you home, and if necessary putting you back in bed."

Carefully Seth lifted himself off the couch. The pain

the movement caused him was mirrored in his eyes. Standing, he leaned heavily on the cane and dragged his leg as he walked.

"Let me help." She hastened to his side.

"I'm perfectly fine without you," he insisted.

Claudia paused and stepped back. "Isn't that the point of this conversation?"

The next days were exhausting. The strain of flu reached epidemic proportions. Both Jim and Claudia were on their feet eighteen hours a day. Claudia traveled from house to house with Jim because the sick were often too ill to come into the city.

When the alarm sounded early the morning of the fifth day, Claudia rolled over and groaned. Every muscle ached, her head throbbed and it hurt to breathe. As she stirred from the bed, her stomach twisted into tight cramps. She forced herself to sit on the edge of the extended hideaway bed, but her head swam and waves of nausea gripped her. A low moan escaped her parted lips and she laid her head back on the pillow. Her fingers groped for the telephone, which sat on the end table beside the bed, and she sluggishly dialed Jim's number to tell him she was the latest flu victim.

Jim promised to check on her later, but Claudia assured him she'd be fine. She just needed rest and some sleep.

After struggling into the bathroom and downing some aspirin, she floated naturally into a blissful sleep.

Suddenly she was chilled to the bone and shivered uncontrollably, incorporating the iciness into her dreams. She was lost on the tundra in a heavy snowstorm, searching frantically for Seth. He was lost, and now she was, too. Then it was warm, the snowflakes ceased and the warmest summer sun stole through her until she was comfortable once again.

"Red?" A voice sliced into her consciousness.

Gasping, Claudia's eyes flew to the one chair in the living room. Seth sat with his leg propped on the ottoman. A worried frown furrowed his brow. Struggling to a sitting position, Claudia pulled the covers against her breast and flashed him a chilling glint. "How'd you get in here?" Her voice came in a hoarse whisper. The lingering tightness in her chest remained painfully constant.

"Jim Coleman let me in. He was concerned about you. I thought it was only right that I volunteer. I owe you one."

"You don't owe me anything, Seth Lessinger, except the right to leave here when the time comes."

He responded with a gentle smile. "I'm not going to argue with you. How are you feeling?"

"Like someone ran over me with a two-ton truck." She leaned against the pillow. The pain in her chest continued, but it hurt less to breathe if she was propped up against something solid. Her stomach felt better, and the desperate fatigue had fled.

"I haven't had a chance to talk to Barbara," he said as his gaze searched her face. "She's been helping Jim and her father the last couple of days. But I'm going to explain things. We're having dinner tonight."

"Seth, please." She looked away. "Barbara loves you, while I . . ."

"You love me, too."

"I'm going back to Seattle, Seth. I was wrong to have ever come North."

"Don't say that, Red. Please."

She slid down into the bed and pulled the covers over her shoulders. Closing her eyes, she hoped to convince him she was going back to sleep.

When she opened her eyes again, the room was dark and Seth was gone. A tray had been placed on the table and she saw that it was a light meal he had apparently fixed for her.

Although she tried to eat, she couldn't force anything down. Her wristwatch had stopped; the world outside her door was dark. There was very little sunlight during the days now, making it almost impossible to predict time accurately. The sun did rise, but only for a few short hours, and it was never any brighter than the light of dusk or dawn.

Claudia was awake when Seth returned. His limp was less pronounced as he let himself into her apartment.

"What are you doing here?" She was shocked at how weak her voice sounded.

"Barbara's got the flu," he murmured defeatedly. "I didn't get to see her for more than a couple of minutes." He sighed heavily as he lowered himself into the chair.

Instantly Claudia was angry. "You beast! You don't have any business here! You should be with her, not me. She's the one who needs you, not me."

"Barbara's got her father. You've only got me," he countered gently.

"Don't you have any more concern for her than this? What if she found out you were here taking care of me? How do you think she'd feel? You can't do this to her—" A tight cough gripped her chest and she shook violently with the spasm. The exertion drained her of what little strength she possessed. Wearily she slumped back and closed her eyes, trying to ignore the throbbing pain in her chest.

Cool fingers rested on her forehead. "Would you like something to drink?"

Nodding was almost more than she could manage. The feeble attempt brought a light of concern to Seth's eyes.

The tea hurt to swallow and she shook her head after the first few sips.

"I'm phoning Jim. You've got something more than the flu." A scowl darkened his face.

"Don't," she whispered. "I'm all right, and Jim's so busy. He said he'd stop by later. Don't bother him, he's overworked enough as it is." Her heavy eyelids drooped, and Claudia returned to a fitful slumber.

Again the warming rays of the sun reappeared in her dream, but this time in a fiery intensity. She thrashed, kicking away the blankets, fighting off imaginary foes who wanted to take her captive.

Faintly she could hear Jim's voice, as if he were speaking in the distance.

"I'm glad you phoned." His tone was anxious.

Gently she was rolled to her side and an icy-cold stethoscope was placed against her bare back. "Do you hear me, Claudia?" Jim's voice asked.

"Of course I hear you." Her voice was shockingly weak and strained.

"I want you to take deep breaths."

Every inhalation burned like fire, searing a path

through her lungs. Moaning, she tried to speak and found the effort too much.

"What is it, man?" Seth was standing above her, his face twisted in grim concern.

Jim Coleman stood at his side and sighed heavily. "Pneumonia."

Chapter Ten

"Am I dying?" Claudia whispered weakly. Cooper and Ashley stood looking down at her from opposite sides of the hospital bed.

Cooper's mouth tightened into a hard line as his gaze traveled over her, the oxygen tubes and intravenous bottles that lined the wall.

"You'll live," Ashley said and responded to the weak smile with one of her own.

"You fool. Why didn't you let me know things hadn't worked out here?" Cooper demanded. "Are you so full of pride that you couldn't come to me and admit I was right?"

Sparks of irritation flashed from Claudia's blue

eyes. "Don't you ever give up? I'm practically on my deathbed and you're preaching at me!"

"I am not preaching," he denied quickly. "I'm only stating the facts."

Jim Coleman chuckled, and for the first time Claudia noticed that he had entered the room. "It's beginning to sound like you're back among the living, and sooner than we expected." Standing at the foot of her bed, he read the chart and smiled wryly. "You're looking better all the time. But save your strength to talk some sense into these folks. They seem to think they're going to take you back to Seattle."

Claudia rolled her head away so that she faced the wall and wouldn't need to look at Jim. "I am going back," she mumbled in a low voice, knowing how desperately Jim wanted her to stay.

A short silence followed. Claudia could feel Cooper's eyes boring holes into her back, but to his credit he didn't say anything.

"You've got to do what you think is right," Jim said at last.

"All I want is to go home. And the sooner the better." Oddly, she had never considered Cooper's penthouse condominium home until now. She'd return to Seattle and rebuild her life. Maybe this was the time to investigate the fancy Swiss medical school her uncle had been so keen about.

"I don't think it's such a good idea to rush out of here," Jim said, and Claudia could tell by the tone of his voice that he'd accepted her decision. "I want you to gain back some of your strength before you go."

"Pastor Reeder introduced himself to us when we arrived. He's kindly offered to have you stay and recuperate at his home until you feel up to traveling," Ashley added.

"No." Claudia's response was adamant. "I want to go back to Seattle as soon as possible. Cooper was right, I don't belong in Nome. I shouldn't have come in the first place."

The words produced a strained silence around the small room. "When will I be discharged, Jim?" Her questioning eyes sought his troubled ones.

"Tomorrow, if you like," he said solemnly.

"I would."

"Thanksgiving Day," Ashley announced.

Claudia's eyes clashed with her friend's. Ashley knew. The day she'd left Seattle, Claudia had told Ashley to expect the wedding around Thanksgiving. And Ashley had teased her, saying Claudia was making sure their anniversary was at a time no one would forget. Recalling the conversation brought a physical ache to her heart. No, she'd said, she wanted to be married around Thanksgiving because she wanted to praise God for giving her such a wonderful man as Seth. Now there would be no wedding. She would never have Seth.

"If you feel she needs more time, Doctor," Cooper began, "Ashley and I could stay a few days."

"No," Claudia interrupted abruptly. "I don't want to stay any longer than necessary." Remaining even one extra day was intolerable.

Claudia closed her eyes, blotting out the world. Maybe she could fool the others, but not Ashley, who gently squeezed her hand. Shortly afterward Claudia heard the sound of hushed voices and retreating footsteps.

The stay in the hospital had been a nightmare from the beginning. Seth had insisted upon flying in another doctor from Anchorage. As weak as she'd been, Claudia had refused to have anyone but Jim Coleman. Jim and Seth had faced each other, their eyes filled with bitter anger. Claudia was sure they'd argued later when she wasn't there to watch.

She had seen Seth only once since that scene, and only to say good-bye. The relationship was over, finished, and Seth had accepted the futility of trying to change her mind.

Pastor Reeder had been a regular visitor. He tried to talk to her about the relationship between Seth, Barbara and herself, but Claudia had stated forcefully that she really didn't want to talk about it. He hadn't brought up the subject again.

Barbara had come once, but Claudia had pretended she was asleep, not wishing to face the woman who would share Seth's life, or make explanations that would only embarrass them.

Claudia relaxed against the pillows, weak after the short visit. Without meaning to, she slipped into a restful slumber.

When she awoke an hour later, Seth was sitting at her bedside. Somehow she had hoped not to see him again. But she felt no overwhelming surprise as she lifted her lashes and their eyes met.

"Hello, Seth," she whispered. Her fingers longed to reach out and touch his haggard face. He looked as if he hadn't slept in several days.

"Hello, Red." He paused and looked away. "Claudia," he corrected. "Cooper and Ashley arrived okay?"

She nodded. "They were here this morning."

"I thought you might want someone with you." He said this with the understanding she wouldn't ever rely on him.

"Thank you. They said you were the one who phoned." Claudia didn't know how she could be so calm. She felt like she had in the dream, lost and wandering aimlessly on the frozen tundra.

Seth shrugged his shoulders, dismissing her gratitude.

"You'll marry Barbara, won't you?"

The hesitation was only slight. "If she'll have me."

Claudia put on a brave smile. "I'm sure she will. She loves you. You'll have a good life together."

Seth neither agreed with nor denied the statement. "And you?"

"I'm going back to school." The smile on her face died and she took in a quivering breath.

He stood and walked across the room to stare out the window, his back to her. He seemed to be gathering his resolve. "I couldn't let you go without telling you how desperately sorry I am," he began before returning to the chair at her side. "It was never my intention to hurt you. I can only beg your forgiveness."

"Don't, please." Her voice wobbled with the effort to suppress tears. Seeing Seth humble himself this way was her undoing. "It's not your fault. Really, there's no one to blame. We've both learned a valuable lesson in this. We should never have sought a supernatural confirmation from God. Faith comes from walking daily with our Lord until we're so close to Him we don't need anything more to know His will."

Until then Seth had avoided touching her, but now he took her hand and gently held it between his two large ones. "When do you leave?"

Even the slight touch of his fingers caused shivers to shoot up her arm. She struggled not to withdraw her hand. "Tomorrow."

He nodded, accepting her decision. "I won't see you again," he said and breathed in deeply. Very gently he lifted her fingers to his lips and kissed the back of her hand. "God go with you, Red, and may your life be full and rewarding." His eyes were haunted as he stood, looked down on her one last time, turned around and walked from the room.

"Good-bye, Seth." Her voice was throbbing and she closed her eyes unable to watch him leave.

"Honestly, Cooper, I don't need that." She was dressed and ready to leave the hospital when Cooper came into her room wheeling a chair. "I'm not an invalid!"

Jim Coleman rounded the corner into her room. "No backtalk, Claudia. You have to let us wheel you out for insurance purposes."

"That's a likely story," she returned irritably. Cooper gave her a hand and helped her off the bed. "Oh, all right, I don't care what you use, just get me to the plane on time." It should be the church, she reminded herself bitterly.

Jim drove the three of them to the airport. Ashley sat in the backseat with Claudia. The two men occupied the front seat.

"This place is something!" Cooper looked around him curiously. "Aren't there any paved roads in Nome?"

"Two," Jim answered as he pulled onto the dirt road that was covered by compacted snow. Although it was almost noon, he used the car headlights. "The road leading to the airport is paved."

"I wish I'd seen the tundra in springtime. From what everyone says, it's a magnificent sight," Claudia murmured to no one in particular. "The northern lights are fantastic. I was up half one night watching them. Some people claim they can hear the northern lights. The stars here are breathtaking. Millions and millions, like I've never seen before. I . . . I guess I'd never noticed them in Seattle."

"The city obliterates their light," Jim explained.

Cooper turned around to look at Claudia. She met his worried look and gave a poor replica of a smile.

"Is the government planning to build any kind of road into Nome?" Ashley questioned. "I was surprised to learn we could only come by plane."

"Rumors float around all the time. The last thing I heard was the possibility of a highway system reaching Nome by the year two thousand."

No one spoke again until the airport was in sight. "You love it here, don't you?" Ashley looked at her with renewed concern, and Claudia glanced out the side window, afraid what her eyes would reveal if she glanced at her friend.

"It's okay," she said, doubting that she'd fooled anyone.

As soon as they arrived, Cooper got out of the car and removed the suitcases from the trunk. Ashley helped him carry the luggage inside.

Jim opened the back door and gave Claudia a hand, quickly ushering her inside the warm terminal. His fingers held hers longer than necessary. "I've got to get back to the office."

"I know. Thank you, Jim. I'll always remember you," she said in a shaky voice. "You're the kind of doctor I hope to be: dedicated, gentle, compassionate. I deeply regret letting you down."

Jim hugged her fiercely. "No, don't. You're doing what you must. Good-bye. I'm sorry things didn't work out for you here. Maybe we'll meet again someday." He returned to the car, pausing to wave before he climbed inside and started the engine.

"Good-bye, Jim." The ache in her throat was almost unbearable.

Ashley was at her side immediately. "You made some good friends in the short time you were here, didn't you?"

Claudia nodded rather than make an explanation that would destroy the fragile control of her composure.

A few minutes later, Claudia watched as the incoming aircraft circled the airstrip. She was so intent that she didn't notice Barbara open the terminal door and walk inside.

"Claudia," she called softly and hurried forward to meet her.

Claudia turned around, shock depleting her face of color.

"Don't leave," Barbara said breathlessly, her hands clenched at her sides.

"Please don't say that," Claudia pleaded. "Seth's yours. This whole thing is a terrible misunderstanding that everyone regrets."

"Seth will never be mine," Barbara countered swiftly. "It's you he loves, it'll always be you."

"I didn't mean for you ever to know."

"If I hadn't been so blind, so stupid, I would have guessed right away. I thank God I found out."

"Did . . . Seth tell you?" she asked in an accusing voice.

Barbara shook her head. "He didn't need to. From the moment Jim brought you into the hospital, Seth was like a madman. He wouldn't leave, and when Jim literally escorted him out of your room, Seth stood in the hallway grilling anyone who went in or out."

For a moment Claudia couldn't speak. A hoarseness was blocking her throat. She put on a false smile and gently shook her head. "Good heavens, you're more upset about my leaving than I am. Things will work out between you and Seth once I'm gone."

"Are you crazy? Do you think I could marry him now? He loves you so much it's almost killing him. How can you be so calm? Don't you care? Don't you honestly care?" Barbara argued desperately. "I can't understand either of you. Seth is tearing himself apart, but he wouldn't ask you to stay if his life depended on it." She stalked a few feet away and pivoted sharply. "It's Thanksgiving," she cried. "You should be thanking God that someone like Seth loves you."

Claudia closed her eyes to the shooting pain that pierced her heart.

"I once said, without knowing it was you, that the girl in Seattle was a fool. If you fly out of here, you're a bigger fool than I thought."

Paralyzed by indecision, Claudia turned to Cooper, her eyes filled with doubt.

"Don't look at me," he told her. "This has got to be your own choice."

"Do you love him, honestly love him?" Ashley asked her gently.

"Yes, oh yes."

Ashley smiled and inclined her head toward the door. "Then what are you doing standing around here?"

Claudia spun around to Barbara. "What about you?" she asked softly.

"I'll be all right. Seth was never mine, I'm only returning what is rightfully yours. Hurry, Claudia, go to him. He's at the office. He needs you." She handed Claudia her car keys and smiled broadly through her tears.

Claudia took a step backward. "Ashley . . . Cooper, thank you. I love you both."

"I'd better be godmother to your first child," Ashley called after her as Claudia rushed out the door.

Seth's building was deserted when Claudia entered. The door leading to his office was tightly shut. She tapped lightly, then turned the handle and stepped inside.

Seth stood with his back to her, his attention centered on an airplane making its way into the darkening sky.

"If you don't mind, Barbara, I'd rather be alone right now." His voice was filled with stark pain.

"It isn't Barbara," she whispered softly.

Seth spun around, his eyes wide with disbelief. "What are you doing here?"

Instead of answering him with words, she moved slowly across the room until she was standing directly in front of him. Gently she glided her fingers over the stiff muscles of his chest. He continued to hold himself rigid with pride. "I love you, Seth Lessinger. I'm yours now and for all our lives."

Groaning, he hauled her fiercely into his arms. "You'd better not change your mind, Red. I don't have the strength to let you go a second time." His mouth burned a trail of kisses down her neck and throat. Claudia surrendered willingly to each caress, savoring each kiss, oblivious to the pain of his punishing hold.

Epilogue

"Honey, what are you doing up?" Seth tied the sash to his robe and wandered sleepily from the master bedroom. Claudia watched her husband with a translucent happiness, her heart swelling with pride and love. They'd been married almost a year now: the happiest twelve months of her life.

Seth moved behind her; his hand closed over her hip before sliding around the full swell of her stomach. "Is the baby keeping you awake?"

Claudia relaxed against him, savoring the gentle feel of his touch. "No, I was just thinking how good God has been to us. A verse I'd read in the Psalms the other day kept running through my mind."

"Did you look it up?"

She nodded, reaching for her Bible. "It's Psalm 16:11.

Thou wilt make known to me the path of life; in Thy presence is fullness of joy; in Thy right hand there are pleasures forever."

Seth tenderly kissed the side of her creamy, smooth neck. "God has done that for us, hasn't He? He made known to us that our paths in life were linked, and together we've known His joy."

Claudia nodded happily, rested the back of her head against his shoulder and sighed softly. "You know what tomorrow is, don't you?"

Seth gave an exaggerated sigh. "It couldn't be our anniversary. That isn't until the end of the month."

"No, silly, it's Thanksgiving."

"Barbara and Jim are coming, aren't they?"

"Yes, but she insisted on bringing the turkey. You'd think just because I was going to have a baby I was helpless."

"Those two are getting pretty serious, aren't they?"

"I think it's more than serious. It wouldn't surprise me if they got married before Christmas."

"It may be sooner than that. Jim's already asked me to be his best man," Seth murmured and his mouth nibbled at her earlobe with little kisses. The two men had long before settled their differences and had become good friends. Claudia had worked for Jim until two additional doctors had set up practice in Nome. The timing had been perfect. Claudia had just learned she was pregnant and she was ready to settle into the role of homemaker and mother.

"I don't know how you can love me in this condition." She turned and slipped her arms around his middle.

"You're not so bad-looking from the neck up," he teased affectionately and kissed the tip of her nose. "Has it been a year, Red?" His gaze grew serious.

She nodded happily and her eyes became tender pools of love. "There's no better time to thank God for each other, and for His love."

"No better time," Seth agreed, his arm cradling her close to his side. "When I thought I had lost you forever, God gave you back to me."

"It was fitting that it should have been Thanksgiving Day, wasn't it?"

"Very fitting," he murmured huskily in her ear, leading her back into their room.

If you enjoyed this book...

then you're sure to enjoy our Silhouette Inspirations Home Subscription Service℠! You'll receive two new Silhouette Inspirations™ novels—written by Christian women, *for* Christian women—each month, as soon as they are published.

Examine your books for 15 days, free.

Return the coupon below, and we'll send you two Silhouette Inspirations novels to examine for 15 days, free. If you're as pleased with your books as we think you will be, just pay the enclosed invoice. Then every month, you'll receive two tender love stories—and you'll never pay any postage, handling or packing costs. If not delighted, simply return the books and owe nothing. There is no minimum number of books to buy, and you may cancel at any time.

Return the coupon today...and soon you'll share the joy of Silhouette Inspirations. Love stories that touch the heart as well as the soul.

Silhouette Inspirations

a love story you'll cherish
$2.25 each

17 ☐ TURN, MY BELOVED
    Helene Lewis Coffer

18 ☐ FOR THE LOVE OF
    MIKE
    Charlotte Nichols

19 ☐ TO LOVE AND
    CHERISH
    Kathleen Yapp

20 ☐ A PROMISE ONCE
    MADE
    Barbara Bartholomew

21 ☐ THANKSGIVING
    PRAYER
    Debbie Macomber

22 ☐ NONE SO BLIND
    Phyllis Halldorson

SILHOUETTE INSPIRATIONS, Department SI/3
1230 Avenue of the Americas
New York, NY 10020

Please send me the books I have checked above. I am enclosing
$_____(please add 75¢ to cover postage and handling. NYS and
NYC residents please add appropriate sales tax.) Send check or
money order—no cash or C.O.D.'s please. Allow six weeks for delivery.

NAME_____

ADDRESS_____

CITY_____STATE/ZIP_____

Silhouette Inspirations

a love story you'll cherish

$2.25 each

LOOK FOR TWO SPECIAL NOVELS OF LOVE AND FAITH EACH MONTH BY SOME OF YOUR FAVORITE ROMANCE AUTHORS

Debbie Macomber   Arlene James
Barbara Bartholomew   Phyllis Halldorson

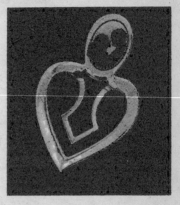